"Thank you for seeing me last minute," she said.

Lyssia had a folder held to her chest, and he nearly laughed at the way she was addressing him. Cold and professional. When only weeks ago he'd had her naked and undone in his bed.

"Of course. You know you don't need a business meeting to see me."

"This is business. I have two important matters to discuss with you."

Dario did feel proud of her then. This was a different side of her. This was the side he always knew was there.

"I want for us to work together. I would like for your resorts to consider carrying my line of home goods. And we are willing to make certain things exclusive to the Rivelli brand."

She shoved one folder at him.

He took it, and began to leaf through it. "I will need some time to..."

"That's fine. But while you consider that, there is one more thing that I need to speak to you about."

"And that is?"

"A custody agreement. You see, I'm pregnant, and I know that it's your baby. So we need to figure out the logistics of that deal as well."

A Diamond in the Rough

Self-made billionaires claim their brides!

To commemorate Harlequin's 75th Anniversary, we invite you to meet the world's most irresistible self-made billionaires!

These powerful men have fought tooth and nail for every success and know better than most how hard life can be. They've overcome significant obstacles, but will they be able to overcome the greatest obstacle of all...love?

Find out what happens in *The Italian's Pregnant Enemy* by Maisey Yates

And watch this space, there are more seductive A Diamond in the Rough heroes coming your way soon!

Maisey Yates

THE ITALIAN'S PREGNANT ENEMY

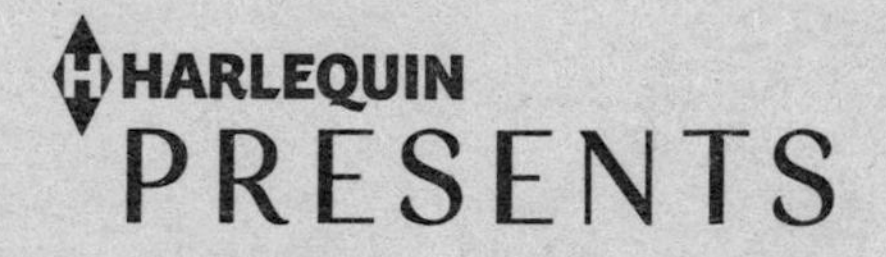

Recycling programs for this product may not exist in your area.

ISBN-13: 978-1-335-59319-1

The Italian's Pregnant Enemy

For questions and comments about the quality of this book, please contact us at CustomerService@Harlequin.com.

Harlequin Enterprises ULC
22 Adelaide St. West, 41st Floor
Toronto, Ontario M5H 4E3, Canada
www.Harlequin.com

Printed in U.S.A.

Maisey Yates is a *New York Times* bestselling author of over one hundred romance novels. Whether she's writing strong, hardworking cowboys, dissolute princes or multigenerational family stories, she loves getting lost in fictional worlds. An avid knitter with a dangerous yarn addiction and an aversion to housework, Maisey lives with her husband and three kids in rural Oregon. Check out her website, maiseyyates.com.

Books by Maisey Yates

Harlequin Presents

Crowned for My Royal Baby
The Secret That Shocked Cinderella

The Royal Desert Legacy

Forbidden to the Desert Prince
A Virgin for the Desert King

Pregnant Princesses

Crowned for His Christmas Baby

The Heirs of Liri

His Majesty's Forbidden Temptation
A Bride for the Lost King

Visit the Author Profile page
at Harlequin.com for more titles.

CHAPTER ONE

LYSSIA ANDERSON HAD a plan. Pink boots, and extremely racy underwear. The boots were useful in the current climate—the ski fields at her father's Alpine resort were freezing. The underwear was not, but that was fine. It wasn't related to the weather. It was related to her plan.

To Carter Westfield, and the growing connection between them.

Her father's new assistant was just…the best. Endlessly caring, so in touch with his feelings, so…sweet. And he was so cute.

Just so cute.

She had never lost her head over a guy before. Not once. And Carter was…

Well, her father sending them on this mission to audit the goings-on at the ski resort was just perfect.

She was thrilled her dad was involving her with the company to begin with. She was at a weird crossroads—one where she was trying to decide what to do with her own company, and what she would do if she did let it go, and she'd finally told her father that it would be nice if there was a space for her at Anderson Luxury Brand Group because she had interned there after all.

He'd listened. He'd told her he would value her input on the condition of the Swiss ski property and that was almost as exciting as the prospect of hooking up with Carter.

They both felt linked, in some ways. She was starting to feel stagnant and there was an underlying discomfort in that stagnation. A feeling that she was treading water when she didn't believe people had that kind of time.

Her mother had died in her twenties. Life wasn't infinite, time wasn't guaranteed.

Onward!

She tightened her parka more firmly around her body—the underwear was beneath layers of warmth, obviously—and pushed open the doors of the lobby. The wind bit into her skin and she fought to keep from reacting to it. She didn't need to go shrieking about the cold in front of the locals.

People already thought of her as a soft heiress, she knew that. A nepo baby. She frequently made online lists of *Twenty-Five Nepo Babies Who Got It All from Their Daddy*, or whatever.

Some nepo baby she was. Her father's luxury vacation empire wasn't even ever going to her. Which was why she'd started her own business three years ago. Which landed her on other, even meaner online lists: *The Least Successful Nepo Babies Squandering Daddy's Money.*

Lyssia Anderson, of the Anderson Luxury Brand Group, runs a tiny boutique interiors business, making furniture and tchotchkes no one asked for.

One has to wonder what a little rich girl who grew up with a pony and an indoor pool knows about what the poor want in their houses. One of her pink couches, which professes to have "custom premium fabrics," retails for over ten thousand dollars.

No wonder she hasn't taken the world by storm.

Not that Lyssia had articles like that memorized.

She was damned if she did and if she didn't. She'd started her own business and it was a source of mockery and disappointment, but if she did nothing she'd be a leech, and if she worked for her father she would just be folded into his dynasty and on and on and on.

She was twenty-three. It wasn't like she was lagging hideously behind. Her company was solvent. It was just that people thought she should be *successful*, so that they could tell her she didn't deserve the success. And until she was, they were going to sneer about how she was losing at life on the easiest setting.

Blah-blah-blah. So many people tore down the achievements of others, but what did they build? Nothing. She'd built something at least.

And she had options.

The problem was, maybe it was true. The business hadn't grown very much in the last few years, and at a certain point she had to wonder if there was truth to what was being said. If she had the backing of her father's name, why was she so mid?

But then her dad seemed to think she was mid too, since she had never been the potential heir to his empire, despite being his only child.

Not when there was Dario.

Something hot churned in her stomach when she thought of him. Dario Rivelli, the antithesis of a nep baby. He'd clawed his way up from nothing, had been taken under her father's wing when he was twenty and making waves in the business world.

He'd gone out on his own, had taken the green housing industry by storm, with groundbreaking build techniques that had quite literally changed the world. Then he'd pivoted into eco-tourism, which had brought him back into her father's life. And her father had…promised him everything.

"Dario Rivelli is the future."

Her father said it like Dario was a god.

But then, her father had always treated Dario like a god. Or perhaps just the son he'd always wanted and never had.

But seriously, he was. Her mom died before her parents could have more kids, and had left this space that contained so many possibilities and no answers. Her dad had been lost in grief, unable to parent, unable to handle Lyssia's emotions and by the time he emerged…

Dario had appeared. Tall and bronze and eminently golden from the inside out.

Lyssia had been keenly away of Dario as competition from the time she was twelve years old. He'd been a grown man and she'd been…jealous of him. Not even mentioning that his dark gaze had always made her feel like something had gone haywire inside of her.

That was how she'd thought of it then. It was how she thought of it now.

The problem was, Lyssia tried. It was only that she wasn't Dario, so what could she do?

Dario might be like a son to her father, but he wasn't like a brother to her. Granted, she did delight in irritating, infuriating and otherwise refusing to be impressed by him. Dario seemed to pride himself on his people management skills. Consequentially, Lyssia refused to be manageable when in his presence.

She'd watched Dario work a room—many times. He was excellent at reading people and figuring out exactly how to behave with them. Lyssia refused to be known. When he looked at her with his cool, dark eyes, she responded with fire. When he treated her to dry, scathing commentary, she responded with spiky words and a placid expression. She knew Dario couldn't tell if she was toying with him, if she was incompetent or an airhead.

When she'd interned at Anderson after she graduated high school she'd been installed as Dario's assistant when he was present at the office and she had absolutely delighted in acting the most unserious person imaginable, much to his irritation.

Of course, in hindsight she could see that hadn't done her many favors.

Act unserious long enough and people believed it.

She wasn't unserious.

She sniffed against the wind—her nose was running—and looked out at the snow, trying to see if there was a vehicle coming for her yet. It was clear and pristine out there. The sky was blue, but there was a band of dark gray clouds looming over the mountains that looked portentous.

Finally, a sleek, black Land Rover pulled up to the curb and Lyssia got inside, her stomach tightening. Carter would be at the chalet she was staying in.

The driver loaded her bags into the back and Lyssia thanked him, even though she could barely hear her voice over the sound of her heart pounding in her head.

She wondered if Carter was expecting this? For her to say it was time for them to take things to the next level. They'd kissed. Like, twice but still. But she wasn't a *child.* And no, she didn't have a lot of physical experience with men, but she was sophisticated enough to know no one was *making out* these days and ending it there.

People were sex positive and liberated. And she was also those things, she had just never been positive she wanted to have sex with anyone, so she hadn't done it. Which was liberation in and of itself, wasn't it?

She wanted to have sex with Carter, though. He made her feel warm and happy, and seen, and wasn't that the thing that was worth waiting for? She thought it might be.

The truth was, he made her feel happy. He made her feel good about herself. That was what she wanted. Someone who made her feel good.

There were just so many hard things. Carter felt easy.

She had been so tempted to text him the whole day but then she'd kept reminding herself to try and be cool. To try and just let it happen. It was very hard to be cool.

As the chalet came into view, her palms got sweaty. Great. No one wanted to be seduced by a woman with sweaty palms. Only then did she think perhaps she should take her mittens off.

But then they stopped and she knew she'd be headed outside again, so the mittens stayed on.

She got out of the car, and the driver handled her bags, bringing them up to the front of the chalet.

Pure adrenaline spiked in her veins. She was going to do it. She wouldn't even wait for it to get dark. That's how sex positive she was.

She went through the door of the chalet, expecting to see Carter there with his laptop. But he wasn't in the grand living area. Nor did he have anything set up in the kitchen. No milk frother. No French press. He kept both on his desk back in Manhattan.

Well, then she could go and take her clothes off. Strip down to her underwear...greet him that way when he arrived.

She laughed out loud in the empty house. No. That was her hard limit.

Still the thought made her feel edgy and a bit... aroused. She didn't hate that.

She went back to the front of the chalet and dragged her bags inside, then began to try and ferret them up the stairs.

She never saw the point in packing light until moments like this, when there wasn't someone around to help her with the heavy lifting.

She grabbed the largest bag first and began to try and drag it up the steep staircase. She struggled, grunted and otherwise made all sorts of very uncute sounds, but finally managed to get it to the top of the stairs.

Then she raced down the stairs and grabbed her other bag, thunking up three steps, then a fourth.

"Trouble, *cara*?"

She shrieked, and released the bag, which slid forward like a sled on the snowy hillside outside, and hit the elegant, gray wood floor below and popped open like a plastic Easter egg, spilling lingerie all over like fruity candy.

Then she looked up and her eyes met *his*.

No.

No this was not happening.

Her heart beat rapidly, like she was a frightened rodent cornered at the edge of her burrow. But she wasn't frightened of Dario Rivelli.

She was *nothing* of him.

So her heart needed to calm the hell down.

"What the…actual…f… What are you doing here?" she asked, hoping she didn't look as red-faced and undone as she felt. As her suitcase looked.

All her underwear.

Her *seduction* underwear.

That Dario was now looking at dispassionately.

He had a cup of coffee in his hand, his white shirtsleeves pushed up to his elbows. The large watch on his wrist somehow served to highlight the muscles on his forearms. She declined to figure out how that worked.

His shoulders were broad and his white shirt rested perfectly over the broad muscles of his chest. It didn't tug at the buttons or anything half so unseemly, yet still seemed far too tight because she shouldn't be able to like, see his muscles? No.

His dark pants were also tailored in a manner she felt to be borderline obscene. She ought not to notice his thigh muscles or…

She forced her gaze back to his face. It was no better. He was practically sneering at her. His dark eyes carrying that hint of mocking humor—as ever. His jaw square, his nose straight as a blade, his lips…

Did not bear reporting on.

At all.

She wasn't looking at his mouth and she never would.

She gathered herself up and walked slowly, very slowly, down the stairs.

"How long have you been standing there?"

He ostentatiously checked his watch. "A couple of minutes."

"You didn't think to announce your presence?" she asked. "Or…help me?"

He lifted one dark brow. "I am a feminist, *cara*. I would never assume you were in need of help without your asking for it."

A feminist her ass.

But she refused to give him a reaction. She outright did. She kept her chin tilted up, her body straight. "Perhaps, once I return my things to their rightful place, you could help."

He moved nearer to her detritus and brushed his foot against the corner of one of her lace nightgown sets as if he was checking a small, limp animal for signs of life.

No dead animals here. It was only her pride that was in danger of dying. That was all.

She slowly—very slowly so as not to seem eager or rushed—bent at the knees and began to shovel her things back into her bag.

He watched her do that, sipping his coffee as if he had all the time in the world. As if he wasn't a very busy, very important billionaire man who had no business being at this chalet when it was a job her father had sent his daughter and his assistant to do. So. Beneath. Him.

But there he was. As if he didn't have a full calendar, demands for interviews every second of the day, and didn't appear in online articles with titles like "Billionaires You'd Actually Like to F—"

"Now, you would like help?" he asked, as soon as she got the zipper down.

"Yes," she said, feeling breathless from exertion and absolutely nothing else. "If you don't mind."

"Not at all. I live to serve you, Lyssia."

She nearly wretched.

He picked up the bag, hefted it over his shoulder, while still holding his coffee in his other hand, and carried it easily up the stairs. Lyssia sniffed and began to trudge up behind him.

She didn't want to sound too interested or eager when she asked her next question. "When are you leaving, Dario?"

Oops.

"I have only just arrived," he said, as he stopped just in front of her bedroom door.

She stopped. "What?"

"I am here for the inspection of the resort."

"What?"

"Your father asked that I come and oversee."

"But Carter and I were supposed to—"

"Your father wanted someone with more seniority to come and inspect, and I offered to do it."

So. She wasn't actually good enough as an inspector for the resort. Of course not. Dario would need to consult and Dario didn't even work for her father anymore. But he was looming about, poised on the brink of an "acquisition" that was really just inheritance, and so his opinion mattered most of all.

All that and Dario was now staying in the same house as her and Carter? Like a big, brooding chaperone?

She could see it now. The real problem wouldn't even be Dario supervising them, it would be the feral monster Dario brought out of her every time they had to share space. She would spend the whole week fighting with him, picking at him, while he sipped his espresso and looked unbothered until he wasn't, until she won her victory. And she'd forget to even kiss Carter, let along bang him.

No. No. She wouldn't let that happen. Dario didn't have to be a barrier. They had their own…whole thing.

Whatever it was. It had nothing to do with what she and Carter had.

"Carter is coming, right?" They could find another room.

Dario lifted a dark brow. "No. He stayed behind. Is that an issue for you, *cara*?"

It felt like a black hole had opened up under her feet. But it refused to swallow her. What was the point of a black hole if it wouldn't even swallow you whole when you were faced with the most horrifying scenario possible?

"Stop calling me *cara*," she snapped. "You don't even like me."

"It's said with irony, are you unaware of irony?"

"A feminist and a comedian, Dario. How did the world get so lucky?"

Here they were. Right in the pocket. Lyssia and Dario and their epic need to go back and forth until one of them broke. It made her forget everything. And everyone. And often the point of what the initial conversation was. Like the whole world fell away and it was just the two of them.

Dario lifted one dark brow and something came alive within her. "Some have said I am a creation of all that the world required. I spontaneously appeared when it was in its darkest hour. And lo."

"The anti-Christ came forth to usher in the end of days?" she asked, sweetly. She thought. A joke, obviously.

"I have not seen any locusts about recently. Though, it may be because of the weather."

"Hmm. Indeed. Locusts are notoriously snow-shy." They stood there in the hall, regarding each other.

Her stomach tightened, her chest getting heavy. It was almost impossible to breathe. Because she hated him so much. So, so much. It was always like this and it never got better. If anything, he had gotten worse in the last couple years.

He was so arrogant.

So tall. It was infuriating. His shoulders were so… so broad and his hands were so big. And she didn't like any of it.

"Thank you," she said, pointedly.

"You do not wish me to place the bag in your room? I know you're accustomed to a full-service life."

She scoffed. "As if you aren't at this point."

It had probably been years since he'd had to see to his own needs. He probably had a driver to drive him in a car and a butler to brush his teeth and a woman to…

Well.

Whatever. She wasn't going to follow that thought up.

She knew full well what women thought of Dario. If there was an event, and he was there, he was sure to have a beautifully polished woman on his arm. A model, an actress, an influencer, a high-society maven, as long as she looked nice in couture.

He didn't have any trouble pulling the kind of woman who looked effortlessly at ease on his arm.

He didn't respond to her jab, which was annoying. They'd had a pretty good streak going. Instead he opened the bedroom door without her permission and brought her bags inside.

She slipped into the room and realized her mistake immediately. The feeling that had been throbbing between them in the hall—the hatred, that's what it was—seemed to expand in here, making it impossible to think, let alone breathe or make a normal facial expression.

He said nothing. He only looked at her. The stark lines of his chiseled face seeming more pronounced just suddenly. Like he was taller, suddenly. Broader, suddenly.

Closer, suddenly.

"All right, *cara*?"

"Yes," she said, her throat scratchy.

Suddenly, she didn't even want to needle him. She just wanted him out of her space.

And she would have it. Tomorrow, she would arrange to have herself moved to a room in the chalet. She was going to finish this job, because as much as she wanted to fly back to Manhattan so she could go ahead and complete her Carter mission, she couldn't let her father think she was putting her personal life over her work. Even if sending Dario to supervise her was an insult.

If she wanted to girl boss her way out of mediocrity, she had to prioritize work when the opportunities came her way.

But she would get in touch with him and make a date for when she got away from here.

"Thanks, Dario," she said.

She hoped the definitive thanks would give him the hint to get on his way.

"Anything for you, of course, Lyssia."

He was mocking her, obviously.

She didn't return volley.

He turned and walked out of the room and left her there to look around the space. It was a lovely room. Big picture windows looked out over the snow. The bright white reflecting beautiful, clean light all around. The bed was modern, low and on a platform, with a white bedspread. The rug right next to a modern, glass fireplace was white reindeer hide, with pale bamboo flooring beneath.

She kicked her shoes off and sighed. The floor was warmed from radiant heat beneath and it felt like luxury. The bathroom was lovely, with a big, deep white tub and slate-gray floating counter.

This would have been a great place to take a bath with Carter.

She sighed wistfully, the romantic scene in her mind feeling cruel now that it wasn't happening. She could so easily imagine sitting with him in the tub, covered in bubbles, sipping champagne.

They would talk about the day they'd had and it would be so…sweet.

She frowned.

And for some reason her brain glitched right then and the picture in her mind tore in two. Behind that image, of herself and Carter with all his golden handsomeness…was Dario.

But in that picture there was no champagne. There were no smiles. No bubbles.

She was across from Dario, naked in the water, his broad chest muscular and covered with dark hair. The look on his face was…angry. Intense. His dark eyes never left her as he moved in to—

"No!" she shouted and leaped back from the empty tub.

What the ever-loving hell was wrong with her?

She needed to get out of this house.

She needed to get away from Dario Rivelli.

The man was her nemesis. And nothing more.

CHAPTER TWO

LYSSIA ANDERSON WAS the most beautiful pain in his ass.

Dario sat in front of the fireplace in the expansive living area of the chalet and pondered his present situation. He shouldn't have agreed to do this. But Nathan Anderson was the closest thing he had to a father—that he acknowledged—in this world, and when the man asked him to do things, he found himself doing them.

No one else on earth could compel Dario to interrupt his schedule to do them a favor.

He thought of Lyssia. Blonde, wide-eyed and hapless, staring at a pile of lingerie at the bottom of the stairs.

A reluctant growl rose in his throat.

The problem with Lyssia was that he could see her. More clearly than she saw herself at times, he had a feeling. She thought he enraged her because she hated him. And perhaps she did. But that wasn't the real reason she puffed up like an angry kitten every time he got too close to her.

Ten years her senior, and vastly more experienced,

Dario did not have a life that lent itself to the sorts of blind spots Lyssia still possessed.

She had clearly imagined she would be having a dirty weekend with her father's pet of a PA. He was the most pathetic puppy of a boy Dario had ever met. Lyssia was obviously besotted with him.

She could control him. That was why.

That was not what Lyssia needed, though. And sadly for her, not what she wanted. Not really. She thought she did, and she might even have some fun with him, but he would never be enough to satisfy her.

He wondered how long it would take her to realize.

That while he truly did find her to be an annoying brat, and he had a feeling she thought he was the most arrogant bastard on the planet, the thing that pulsed between them whenever they clashed was not merely hatred, but desire.

He could remember the moment she'd become a problem.

He'd known Lyssia since she was a child. But he'd only had a vague concept of her. She'd been the little creature running around Nathan's home on his rare visits there, but he'd only ever seen her in passing. After her mother's death, Lyssia had begun to spend more time in the office. A sullen teen with questionable fashion sense, she'd often been found lying upside down on a couch in the lobby of her father's multibillion-dollar company, like an insolent throw pillow, or sitting in her father's office chair while he was in a meeting.

At eighteen, she'd started an internship there, and he'd been forced to interact with her. At that point,

Dario no longer worked at Anderson's. In fact, his company had acquired it under the umbrella of his other interests, as part of Nathan's retirement plan. They had a ten-year contract that would slowly begin to turn the operation over to Rivelli Holdings, integrating financial systems and other areas of the company over time while trying to retain as much staff as possible.

Nathan was very conscientious about such things, and Dario appreciated it because he wasn't certain if he would have been.

He'd come to Manhattan an angry thirteen-year-old who'd lied about his age to get a contract on a cruise ship sailing between Europe and the US. He'd seen it as a way out of Rome, and he'd wanted out badly.

And he'd gotten what he wanted. He'd spent the first years of his life helpless. After the worst had happened, he'd realized he had two choices. To sit down and die, or to use the breath he had in his body to ensure he would never be helpless again.

He hadn't been. He'd gotten off the ship and disappeared into the city. He'd fashioned a new identity for himself. Gotten papers. Gotten work. In kitchens, in restaurants. Finally, in hotels. He had been tall for his age, handsome and in possession of natural charisma.

Lyssia might disagree, but most other people found him charming.

He'd used that to his advantage. He was an expert at reading people. At mimicking manners and voices. He'd worked to leave most of his accent behind. He had just enough to sound delightfully foreign when it suited him. He'd educated himself by speaking to the people around him. He'd learned to talk, dress, act and comport himself as a member of the upper class he saw come into the hotels he worked in.

He'd gotten a job at the Anderson's on Fifth Avenue when he was seventeen. By the time he was nineteen, he was the manager. At twenty-one he was managing all of the hotels in North American. At twenty-four he'd been the global strategist for the brand and had grown the company astronomically, earning himself a reputation and a vast fortune.

At twenty-five he'd gone out on his own, with his mentor's blessing. He'd bought a struggling hotel chain and had turned it around, had made it a business, rehabbing old resorts, before beginning to build new resorts that catered to eco tourists.

He'd been a billionaire before his thirtieth birthday.

It was then that Nathan asked him to consult on making his resorts as close to net zero as possible, and they'd come up with the idea of his eventual takeover.

It was the closest thing to family Dario had ever known.

The closest thing to an inheritance he could have imagined. It wasn't the value that mattered. It was the trust.

He'd never had anything like that before, and he would never take it for granted.

But that had meant that even though he was not an employee of Anderson, he still had a lot of business to do with Anderson. Which meant he was exposed to Lyssia. Often.

At the time he'd had an office in the Anderson

Group building in Manhattan and Lyssia was his assistant when he was in the office.

He'd lost track of the amount of coffees he'd been delivered with her patented pout.

She had the most beautiful mouth. Her top lip was fuller than the bottom lip, pale pink. Her lips curved down at the corners. It was an eternal sulk.

She would bring it in and bend over his desk, smelling like sunshine and something sweet, and very expensive.

He'd been twenty-eight at the time and not interested in teenagers, even if they were technically adults in the eyes of the law.

Until one day she'd brought a coffee, and she'd tripped.

He'd jumped up out of his chair and grabbed her forearm, preventing her from crashing headfirst into the carpet, and the coffee had gone all over the front of his shirt.

She'd paused for a moment, frozen.

Then she'd looked up at him, and the sulky corners of her mouth had turned upward. She'd smiled. And then she had laughed.

Loud and long, like music, as he'd held her, wearing a sodden shirt.

He'd set her back on her feet. It felt as if the room had turned, while they'd stayed standing right in the same place they'd been at before.

But it had forced him to see her from a new angle and he had never been able to unsee it. For five years, he'd been held captive by her beauty.

But Lyssia was the only woman in the world who didn't find him charming.

Even if she did, she was the daughter of his mentor and he had no desire to negatively impact that relationship by touching his baby girl. God forbid.

Dario wanted neither marriage, nor children.

Lyssia would want both. And a golden retriever. As her husband and her pet.

He stood up from his place by the fire and walked into the kitchen, getting a pot of soup out and putting it on the burner. Then he found a boule of bread and sliced it, taking out a large block of butter as well. A simple dinner, but fine for him.

He loved luxury, he could not deny it. Excess would never fail to make the streets feel farther and farther behind him. But he also didn't mind simple food, simple evenings.

He took his bowl of soup to the table by the window and looked out at the scene. It was twilight, and all the snow was brilliant blue.

Silence was a luxury. In Rome a man could scarcely achieve it, even with millions. It had been far beneath a boy who lived on the streets.

Silence was his favorite indulgence.

"Dario."

He lifted his head and saw his little blonde problem standing in the doorway. She had shattered his silence. Her hair was wet and she was wearing a white T-shirt that fell down to her knees, with a pair of sweatpants underneath.

"Did you have a bath, Lyssia?"

Her blue eyes widened, her cheeks going pink. "No. A shower. Why?"

Why indeed? Because he'd asked the first question that had come to his mind. Never a good idea. "Just concerned you were engaged in some sort of social media challenge where you stuck your head in a snowbank for clout."

"As I'm known to do," she said, dryly. "Is there dinner?"

She expected him to have handled dinner, of course. And he had. She was very spoiled, and he had a feeling she had no real idea that she was. But watching her careen about with her luggage she couldn't manage, only to emerge hours after he'd left her in her room looking hungry and fragile, he wondered if the child could survive for five minutes on her own, even if she was in a luxury chalet.

"Yes, of course. Soup and bread. Feel free to avail yourself."

He should leave. He didn't.

Lyssia returned a moment later with a bowl of soup and a stack of bread on a plate.

She sat at the table across from him and she looked… disappointed to see him there.

"Sad that I'm not your boyfriend?" he asked.

Her cheeks turned pinker still. "Carter isn't my boyfriend."

"But you expected to meet him here and stay with him."

"Yes," she said.

"He didn't tell you about the change?"

She opened her mouth, then closed it, and opened it again. Like a very small guppy. "Well, in fairness to him, I don't think he knew I was hoping for this to be more than business."

A funny thing about Lyssia. She didn't lie to him. She might jab at him verbally, she might fight and hiss and spit, but she didn't lie. Then, he didn't lie to her either. Why? They drove each other mad. He had no reputation to preserve with her, and she none with him. Dropping bombs was more fun than crafting narratives. And they both seemed to take that tactic.

"How long does it take to send a text?" he asked.

"He's busy," she said, her teeth clenched.

"Have you spoken to him?"

"Not yet. But I haven't texted him either."

"You could call."

"I will tomorrow," she said.

Interesting. He would have thought that thwarted young lovers wouldn't be able to spend even a moment apart. Unless they were not lovers yet. That could very well be.

She'd obviously intended for this week to change things, in that case.

"It seems poor form to leave a woman guessing."

"Maybe people in your generation need to be in constant contact."

His generation. He couldn't help himself. He laughed. "*Cara*, a man who wants a woman makes it plain, regardless of his generation. If he does not, then he is not a man, and he does not want you."

"First of all that's very gender essentialist, and second of all, that isn't true. People's lives don't revolve around romance, you know. They have to prioritize themselves too. Carter has likely had a long day dealing with my father—I used to assist both him and you so I know how blessedly annoying it can be."

"Yes, I'm known for that."

"And," she continued, "he probably has to engage in some self-care before going to bed and preparing for work tomorrow."

"Self…care?"

"Yes. Lighting a candle, listening to Enya, doing a sheet mask."

Her expression was entirely bland. He couldn't tell if she was being serious or not.

"I do not understand how this is care?"

"OMG, of course you don't."

She was goading him. He could do one better.

"Lyssia, if I had a beautiful woman waiting for my call I would call her. What is a lit candle for if not to gaze at your lover in firelight?" Her eyelashes fluttered. She looked away from him. He felt something wicked tighten his gut. Something he knew full well he shouldn't indulge. "What is music for, if not a soundtrack to which you might seduce your lover?"

Her eyes had gone glassy and she was looking at him now. "And the sheet mask?"

"I do not know what that is."

"It's for your skin."

"I still don't know what it is."

"It makes your skin look…glowy."

He laughed. "Now that really is useless. Nothing

makes a woman's skin glow better than the aftereffects of lovemaking. A man who needs a *sheet mask* is not an accomplished lover."

She sounded like she was wheezing. "In this case it's for his skin, not mine."

"Either way."

"Well, that's how you see things," she said. "People now might argue that's toxic."

"To be thought of at all times? Desired at all times?"

"Yes. It's not that deep."

He huffed a laugh. "Then why bother with it?"

It was a disingenuous question. His relationships were never deep. But she didn't seem like she would be that sort of person. She was…

It was difficult to describe Lyssia, who seemed to take many of life's luxuries for granted, but was also emotional, passionate and compassionate…in certain ways.

She could also be scathing, sharp and sarcastic. With him. Only ever with him.

"You're indoctrinated by Fairy-Tale Culture," she said. "Entertainment aimed at children that centers on romantic relationships and only depicts happy endings containing conventional romances have poisoned you."

He did not bother to ask her why she thought he might have consumed such media. "Yes, Lyssia, that is my Achilles' heel. I am an old-fashioned romantic."

He stared at her, his face perfectly blank.

She stared back and frowned. "Are…you?"

She thought him humorless, and as a result could never really tell when he was simply being dry.

He did wonder how much of that she turned back on him.

"I've been planning my wedding since I was a small boy."

"You...have?"

He declined to answer.

"My point is," she said. "Just because you don't understand something doesn't mean it's *less than*."

"Ah. A good thing you told me since you did not, in fact, make your point. My point, *cara*, is that just because you have an internet connection it does not make you an expert."

"I think I can claim to be the expert on the situationship that I'm in."

He frowned. "What is that word?"

"It's like a relationship but not as binding." She lifted her spoon out of her bowl and swirled it in the air. "A situation that is relationship adjacent."

"I should have invested in space travel so I could leave this planet."

"So pressed," she said, putting her spoon back down into her soup.

"If I seem *pressed* to you it is merely because I'm trying to explain to a spoiled rich girl why she should value herself a bit more, when from my perspective you should value yourself innately, given the advantages you have."

She frowned. "You think by being with Carter I'm not valuing myself?"

"It seems like it to me."

"And also, why should I innately value myself exactly? Because my dad loves some random dude more than he loves me, so much so that he's sold off my inheritance to said man?"

He was the random man, he realized. And this was the first he'd heard of her feeling…angry about him taking over Anderson. Also, she was being well provided for. So he knew she was being over the top by saying this; he just wasn't certain how much of it was true and how much was part of her brand of drama. "I was unaware your father was leaving you penniless."

She scoffed. "He isn't. But he's turning the company over to you and he never once asked me if I wanted…"

"Are you an accomplished businessperson in the hospitality industry?"

"Well…no."

"Did you work your way up from nothing through every level of hotel work?"

"I…no."

"Have you ever had an hourly wage job in your entire, privileged life?"

"No. But."

"I am more qualified than you are. If you had ever been interested in taking over your father's empire, then you would have worked for it, wouldn't you?"

"I was eighteen when he made the decision to give it to you. I barely had a chance. And anyway, it isn't about whether or not I should be in charge, or if you're more…qualified. It's just… If I were his son would he have done this?"

It was a fair question, he supposed. But as his relationship with his own father was so much more toxic than she could ever imagine, he'd never once turned over this sort of philosophical ridiculousness.

"I was on a ship bound for America when I was *thirteen*."

"With the pilgrims?" she asked.

He laughed. "Very funny. I was working in hospitality then, and I continued to do so. My course was set by the time I was eighteen. I don't view age as an excuse."

He wasn't entirely sure how much of his personal biography she knew. It would be entirely on brand for her to be completely studied in it, yet look at him with wide eyes and say she'd had no idea.

"Have you not read my biography?"

"The one where you had a literal sea monster's baby? Oh, sorry, I think that was some weird fanfic I found on the internet."

"Did you write it?"

She smiled. "I did write you into a story of mine when I was twelve or so."

"The handsome prince."

"No. You were the villain."

He smiled. Slowly. "Sadly for you, Lyssia, I think you're drawn to a villain."

She laughed, and then inhaled her bread on accident and began hacking while laughing. "Please! *Please.* I do not like villains. I like nice men with nice hair and French presses on their desks. Who ask how my day is and who kiss like summer rain. And who will appreciate my underwear, not stare at them like they're flat animals."

And just like that his mind went back to that underwear, scattered about the floor, not like *flat animals*, whatever the hell that meant, but like forbidden confetti for a party he had no business wanting to attend.

And yet she vexed him. Tormented him. When nothing else on the earth dared to.

"Has he called?" he asked.

Lyssia's mouth dropped. Her cheeks went scarlet. "I've already told you..."

"Careful, your mask is slipping."

Her eyes narrowed. "There is no mask, Dario. We aren't all committed to facades."

"So this is you, then."

"This is me," she said, standing from the table. "I am exactly what you see here. I am the ever-underestimated Lyssia Anderson."

"Sheet masks and self-care."

"If that's all you got out of the last couple hours, the problem is you, not me."

It wasn't. She was smart and funny, and angry. Very angry. At him, he thought, but also at her father. He knew she felt undermined by his presence. But the truth was, Dario felt like Nathan was taking care of Lyssia by ensuring the business went on, and healthily. Lyssia had many shares in the company in her name, and she would be getting money when the acquisition went through. Her pride was wounded, perhaps, but he couldn't see Lyssia seriously wanting to run a major corporation.

The problem with Lyssia was she didn't know herself.

"You are the most committed to facades, Lyssia. You don't even know what's beneath your own mask."

"That is some impressive arrogance."

"Let me impress you further. You don't want a nice man. You want a man who will tell you when you're being a brat. You want a man who will ask you how your day has been, and if it's been bad, he'll do something about it. Even unto turning the city upside down to right a wrong against you. You want a man who will call you. You don't want warm summer rain. You want a hurricane. You don't want a job at your father's company because you want to make a name for yourself, but you have to stop being so stubborn about how you want that success to look. And until you can admit that to yourself you'll be stuck in this insipid in-between space with an insipid in-between man. And you deserve more, Lyssia."

He had moved nearer to her while he was talking and the space between them was charged. Lyssia's breathing changed. It was short and sharp, her eyes searching his face as if she might find answers there.

"You don't...you don't know me," she said.

"But I do. I've known you for a very long time."

She shook her head. "You know what you think you see, and nothing more."

"No, Lyssia. I see you. The you not even you see."

She took a step toward him and all went silent. "Does that mean I see you? Am I the only one who sees that you're more arrogance than substance?"

He reached out and gripped her arm and the touch was like an electric shock. He released her, as instantly as he took hold.

She was stunned into silence.

The truth was, Lyssia Anderson was a brat.

And he should not struggle with the desire to take her in hand and turn her tantrums into sighs of pleasure.

But even now, he did.

“I'm going to bed,” she said, her voice thin.

“Yes,” he said. “A good idea.”

Tomorrow she would move back to the main hotel and she wouldn't be his problem. He could do his work without distraction.

That was all he really wanted.

CHAPTER THREE

When Lyssia woke up the next morning, all was quiet. The kind that felt like a weighted blanket, settling over her all warm and comforting.

She didn't want to move. Didn't want to disturb her own relaxation. But then she remembered. Dario.

Her eyes popped open. She needed to get out of here. She was stuck in this house with that man.

She needed to call Carter, and she needed to get a room at the main lodge. Wouldn't be an issue. Easily solved.

She tumbled out of bed and looked at the clock. She was jet-lagged, so it was an odd time, and not a good one to call Carter. Too bad.

She picked up the phone on the nightstand, a landline that was connected to the front desk. There was no tone.

That was weird.

She pushed a button to try and wake the phone up. If that was how such things worked. It didn't seem to be.

She pushed a button again. And then again.

Nothing seemed to work.

She growled. Well, she would use her phone to look up the number to the front desk, then.

She would take some coffee first, though. She hoped that there was space available for her. Because while she was keen to get the overview of the property done, she was even more keen to get out of the presence of Dario.

He just…

He got under her skin. He had been so rude and condescending last night. Lecturing her about her relationship with Carter.

And all right, maybe they hadn't given their relationship rules or parameters or a title. But it was there. She knew it.

She let herself think, for just a minute, that he might even be the one. That he was actually Prince Charming.

It made her heart lift.

Maybe he was the one who would see her for who she was. The one who would put the slipper on her foot…

She was a product of society. She might know full well that fairy-tale syndrome was a problem, but that didn't mean she hadn't taken some of the motifs on board and internalized them. And sometimes, just a little bit, she indulged in a fantasy or two that was maybe a bit more sweeping and romantic than she had pretended while talking to Dario.

You want the villain...

She didn't.

And, oh, how she hated Dario.

She really did.

She'd been speechless with it last night when he'd reached out and grabbed her arm…

How dare he?

How dare he criticize sweet, lovely Carter and… and…

She looked at herself in the mirror and frowned. What she had ended up wearing to bed last night was not cute. It was not like any of the gorgeous things in her suitcase.

All those beautiful, sexy things. She had been so intent on having that. On playing the role of seductress.

She had so looked forward to being wanted.

Because at least with Carter she felt like something was there. Like he enjoyed having her around. At least with him she didn't feel like she was fitting through cracks. Her father's daughter, but only a little bit. Because somehow Dario was more his child than she was in many ways. Or perhaps the child he wished he'd had.

And he certainly wasn't like a brother to her.

No. Not in the least.

He didn't even *like* her. He didn't even…

Right then, her eyes went past the mirror, into the bathroom and landed on the baths.

Lord.

She was not going to think about that again. It had been an aberration. Dario was… He was attractive. She supposed. If you were into that kind of thing. To that macho, old-school, extremely masculine sort of beauty.

He was also a brick wall.

And anyone who was with him was going to spend most of her life flinging herself at that wall. No thanks.

She already felt unwanted and invisible half the time.

Of course, the truth was, when she thought about seducing Carter she thought about what she would wear. What she would do. How beautiful she would feel.

She hadn't spent much time thinking about what he might do to her. Even when she had tried to have a fantasy about being in the tub with him, it had been about companionship.

That image of Dario hadn't been companionable at all. It had been about his hands on her skin, his lips on her neck…

She squeezed her thighs together and made a short, frustrated sound as a lightning bolt of sensation centered there. She did not need that.

In any variation.

Even though she was not fond of her pajama situation, she decided it didn't matter what she looked like, and went downstairs on the hunt for caffeine. That way, she could actually think, and not hallucinate about things she absolutely did not want to hallucinate about. Her imagination did not have her consent to go putting images like that in her brain.

She stood in front of the coffee maker, and saw it was much more complicated than she had anticipated. A manual espresso machine.

Great.

"Need some help, *cara*?"

She turned around, her heart thundering. "I don't need any help."

"You look as if you do."

The bath images came to her mind again.

He did not have the right to look so good this early in the morning. He was wearing a tight white T-shirt and black sweatpants and she could see every muscle through that T-shirt.

She would do well to remember that he was an asshole, and just because she had noticed that he was attractive did not mean that she needed to focus on him being attractive.

It mattered much more how somebody was on the inside, anyway. Every child knew that.

That was kindergarten stuff.

Sadly, when she looked at him she did not feel kindergarten stuff.

But on the inside, he was mean. So it didn't matter how beautiful he was. It didn't matter that his abs were visible through a T-shirt. Abs couldn't talk to you about your day. Couldn't offer you emotional support.

"I'm good."

He shifted, and her eyes went to his muscular thighs.

They could not listen to her talk about her day either, but would probably be useful in lifting her up and carrying her around. She imagined the way that he had thrown her suitcase over his shoulder last night. How much more easily could he pick her up and…

What was that about? She was not that woman. She was not the kind of woman who lost her head over raw masculinity. She wasn't… The truth was, she wanted to be close to Carter. It wasn't really about sex. It was, but it wasn't. For some reason, her thoughts of Dario seemed to be a bit too much about sex.

She needed to get out of here.

"The phone in my room wasn't working."

"No," he said. "It wouldn't be."

"Why wouldn't it be?"

"Have you looked out your window?"

"No."

"You might want to do that."

She scampered from the room and went into the dining area, where there was a large set of corner windows. She looked out and she saw nothing but white.

"Um... What?"

"We are snowed in," he said.

"No," she said. "How could that be? This is a modern luxury resort!"

"Yes, and it exists in a world with weather," he said, his tone maddeningly dry.

"But this wasn't called for."

"Apparently there was a major event last night. A wind change that blew a storm front this direction. It dumped an unprecedented amount of snow by here."

"You can't mean that we're actually snowed in in this house. You mean like onto the mountain."

"I do not," he said. He strode from the room, without saying anything, and she followed him. As fast as her legs could take her.

He opened the front door to the outside, and there it was. An absolute wall of snow. Blocking the way out.

"We're going to die!" she shouted.

She was maybe being overdramatic, but she was doing it to try and make herself feel like it was a performance and not…a very real fear and oh, she was going to die a virgin.

She looked up at Dario and decided that was a very bad line of thinking.

But also her mother really had died in her twenties. Young and beautiful and with a whole life ahead of her…except she hadn't had anything ahead of her at all.

"I don't think we will," Dario said. "Die that is. Considering we are on a powerful backup generator that has stored enough solar power to run for a week, and there are food stores not just in the fridge, but in a basement area. I have already made sure that we are fine. We are still able to use satellite internet. Though, wired services are down in the area."

"This is… This is unreal. Unbelievable. There's no way. I can't be snowed in here with you."

"But you are," he said.

"No," she said. "I won't have it. I was supposed to be here with Carter."

"Alas," he said. "I can see how you would've found him to be a more agreeable roommate. But it is not to be."

"I…"

She suddenly felt overwhelmed. By everything. By the betrayal of the weather, her own imagination and Dario himself.

"If you weren't such an unpleasant bastard," she said. "Perhaps this wouldn't be so upsetting."

"I'm sorry that you find me to be so trying," he said.

"But the truth of the matter is, we are adults, and we will figure out how to weather the situation. As soon as the sun rises in New York I will call your father and let him know that you're safe."

"He will be much more concerned about your safety, Dario. And I think you know that. I'm not the heir-apparent to his empire."

"Neither am I. I'm the man who acquired it. You seem very fixated on the idea that I inherited something. I bought it."

"It's all the same, isn't it?"

"It isn't. Because your father was given money in exchange for the business, and who do you think is going to get that money?"

She felt like she had been slapped.

"It doesn't…"

"It does," he said. "Your father gave you freedom. You have never shown the slightest bit of interest in running the company, and he knows that. Imagine, walking around feeling so wounded when your father cares for you so very clearly. I cannot imagine such a thing. Your father is one of the best men that I have ever known. Your determination to see him as an enemy is ridiculous."

"Is it? He has certainly never given me any reassurance about the situation. I am obviously of the lowest priority to him."

"He has given you…"

"Do you not understand that there is…more to being someone's family, to being their father, than giving them money? I thought when he sent Carter and I here this week it was a gesture. That it was him finally acting like I had a brain and that I was capable, but it isn't. Because here you are. You, his golden boy."

"You are of the highest priority to him. Why do you think my intention is to let him know of your safety the minute he awakens?"

"You're unknowable."

"Am I? I think that actually I've made myself fairly clear. You're the one having a tantrum because you are stuck with someone that you have known all of your life, as if you have been thrown in a prison cell with a stranger."

"My week is ruined," she said.

"What a trial for you. To be stuck in a luxury chalet. Thank you for reinforcing my opinion of you, Lyssia."

She felt stung by that. She was upset. Did she have a right to be? She was supposed to be here with someone she actually cared about, someone who cared about her. And instead she was stuck with a man who disdained her. It was fair to be upset about that. It was fair to be upset about the fact that she was having intrusive thoughts about being naked with him when she wanted to punch him in the face. He didn't listen. He was so arrogant his ego practically needed its own chalet.

"They'll come and fix it, right?" she asked.

"I'm sorry, what do you mean by they will come and fix it?" he asked.

"Snowplows," she said.

"I have a feeling that this is a bit beyond just calling in a snowplow."

"Why… Then I'll dig out myself."

He looked at her and said nothing. Then he turned and walked away, leaving her standing there in front of the wall of light, the cold radiating off of it sending chills through her body. He returned a moment later, with a gleaming silver spoon in his hand.

"I know that normally you keep this in your mouth. But perhaps you might make use of it as a tool to tunnel out?"

She grabbed the spoon and threw it across the room. "You're unbelievable," she said. "You're making fun of me."

"Yes, I am. I have been since you arrived, in fact." He shrugged. "Actually, I've been making fun of you for several years, it's only that you don't think I have a sense of humor."

"Because you're unpleasant. Because you're ridiculous and…"

"Please, save your energy," he said, closing the door. "All is well here. And I do not foresee there being any problems."

The adrenaline of the situation was beginning to wear off and she was starting to think a little bit more clearly. He was speaking very confidently, but the truth was… He didn't know any of those things. What if they did lose power? What if the generator wasn't sufficient? What would happen to them then?

"Lyssia," he said softly. "Do not work yourself up. You're fine. You will be all right. Nothing bad is going to happen to you."

He was being nice now and that was almost worse.

Because he really didn't get her. And she shouldn't be upset by that.

He didn't understand that she was frightened because the world was unforgivably random and violent. He didn't understand she was hurt by her father because she had never, not once, been the number one person in his life. It was her mother, and then Dario, and never her.

"You don't know that," she said. "You don't know that nothing bad will happen. But if the power goes out..."

"We will make a fire."

"Do you know how to do that? Can you actually get to any wood?"

"I grew up on the streets of Rome," he said. "And no, I was not often caught in blizzards, but I know how to survive. This will be no different. It is not even a challenge. We are in a luxury chalet."

She knew that. She knew it as part of the legend of Dario Rivelli. Up from the streets! A tale of survival and hardscrabble work ethic. Bootstraps, bootstraps, etcetera. But the problem was, she had never really sat and pictured the Dario she knew living that life. He felt so removed from it. But when he'd said that just now she had pictured him on the streets. Alone. Dario, a small boy out fending for himself. Was that really what that meant? How long had he been on the streets?

"How many years?"

"I'm sorry?" he asked. "It's pretty well stocked but I doubt we have years."

"No. How many years were you on the streets of

Rome?" He stared at her and she stared back. "It gets tossed around like…like it's just evidence of your survival skills or your exceptionalism but I'm…absolutely freaked out about spending five minutes in this place and you're right. It's heated and safe and fine. How many years?"

Something shifted in his gaze and it physically hurt her to see it. "Perhaps only a year or so on the actual streets?"

He was lying. He knew how many nights. Down to the exact number of them, she was certain. "I eventually got work, which allowed me shelter, even if it would be considered subpar by many. Once I could work I could live. It saved me."

"Were you… Were you afraid?" She would have been.

"Of course."

"Did you have a house before that? What happened?"

"Is this twenty questions about tragic backstories now, Lyssia?"

She shrugged. "We're snowed in."

"Aren't you afraid of the snow?"

"Yes, but I want to know."

Anyway, his confidence had soothed her. She felt slightly calmer now, but also a bit rueful, because he was the one who had calmed her.

She hadn't ever appreciated before that it was an asset to be near a man like him who had experienced certain things. The truth was, she didn't have experience with much.

She hadn't really been conscious of that until now. She had never thought of it as a lack, or something that would give her a deficit. She did feel young then. Next to him. She did feel sheltered and cosseted and unaware. In a way she never had before.

It made her… Feel respectful of him. It was a strange experience, and she didn't like it. And yet she was in no real position to push back and be bratty. Mostly because she had already overplayed her hand quite a bit. But also, because he was the person offering to keep her alive during this unexpected blizzard.

"Yes, I had a house. A normal house. And then things changed. As I think you know life often does."

"What happened?"

"The usual sorts of sad things," he said, his tone clipped.

He wasn't being honest. Because Dario was always honest. It wasn't a lie, necessarily, she had a feeling it was all very sad, but she also had the sense that there was something underlying it.

"Come," he said. "I'll make you coffee."

"Why are you being nice?"

"Who said I was being nice? Perhaps I simply want you quiet."

That was how she found herself hooked up on a fluffy round white chair in the living room, waiting for him to deliver her a hot cup of coffee.

He bestowed it upon her and she was struck by the strange irony of the moment. How many times had she brought him coffee in his office?

She looked up at him, and decided that was a mistake. There was something in his dark eyes that made her stomach feel tight.

Then she reached out and took the cup of coffee from his hand. Their fingertips brushed. In spite of herself, she felt that same arrow of pleasure right there between her thighs that she felt when she thought about being in the bathtub with him up in her room. Correction, she hadn't thought about it. Her brain had implanted the thought into her consciousness. She had not thought of it on her own. No way.

And now something was happening to her here.

"Thank you," she said.

She sat there in the living room brooding for the next couple of hours, and then she heard his deep voice coming from the other room. He was talking to her father. Assuring him that everything was all right.

She couldn't hear the exact words, but she could hear the melody of his voice.

It was deep, and reassuring.

She felt bad he'd called her dad first, actually. She should have done it but she was all tangled up in hurt over him sending Dario in the first place.

You're glad Dario is here now...

And that was when she realized that she should probably give Carter a video call.

She also realized that she was hungry.

And she wanted to talk to him, so why shouldn't she?

She pushed aside all of the things that Dario had said to her last night.

It wasn't Dario's business what she was doing. A

side effect of being snowed in was that she happened to be in his vicinity. But that was not her choice. She grabbed her phone and walked into the kitchen, setting it on the counter as she pushed in the numbers to make a video call, reaching for some bread from the cupboard as the phone rang.

She heard the tone that indicated he had picked up, and she looked down at the screen, smiling. He had his phone sitting on his desk, but she could tell that he looked happy to hear from her.

"Hi, Carter," she said.

"Hi. How is Italy?"

"Snowy," she said. "Actually, I'm snowed in at the chalet with Dario."

"Oh," he said, sounding... She couldn't quite pinpoint it. Was he regretful because he wasn't here? Because if he had come, then they would be snowed in together.

"I know, right? So insane."

"Was it even in the forecast?"

"No," she said, getting down a jar of peanut butter. She began to make a sandwich, standing above her phone. "Dario says that the generator should work? But it's honestly a bit unnerving. There's snow all the way up the windows."

"You're completely trapped with..."

He didn't say Dario's name, he only made a face.

"Don't worry," said Lyssia. "I think he only eats children and small animals. I should be safe."

"Perhaps." She jumped, then turned around sharply and saw Dario standing in the doorway.

"I'm on the phone," she said.

His eyes flicked down to where her phone rested on the counter.

"Is that… Being on the phone?"

"Yes," she and Carter said at the same time.

Dario walked over and peered down into her screen. "Who wishes to speak to someone by talking up their nostrils?"

"It's… It's called making face-to-face connections and being authentic," she said.

Then she picked the phone up and grabbed her newly assembled peanut butter and jelly sandwich. Then she hopped out of the room past Dario.

"I wish you were here," she said.

Because she did decide to go ahead and put herself out there, even though Carter hadn't said anything to the effect of being sorry he wasn't there.

She had thought that she would be losing her virginity this week. Not that virginity mattered. It was a social construct. But a person was allowed to think it was a little bit momentous that if they had never driven a car before they were going to drive a car for the first time. It wasn't like it fundamentally changed you or anything, but still. It was okay to have nerves and excitement and anticipation about something like that.

So too, with the virginity.

"I'm sorry that you're stuck there with Dario."

She realized that he didn't say that he was wishing he was there.

And she wouldn't have worried about that, she wouldn't have worried about that at all if it wasn't for what Dario had said last night. The way that he had made a big deal out of whether or not a man was indicating he wanted her as much as she wanted him.

But that didn't matter. It was a fundamentally uninteresting thing.

Because the way that she felt about Carter was about her. About what she wanted. It didn't need to be twisted up in a competition for who felt the most deeply. If she wanted him, then that was what mattered, right?

She wasn't needy.

"Well, it's a good thing you have power," said Carter.

"I know, right? The phone lines are down, and if we didn't have power then we wouldn't have internet of any kind. Well, I suppose we would be able to hook up cell towers for a few hours, but then the phone would die."

"A definite problem."

"For sure."

She took a bite of her sandwich, and right then, all the lights around her went out.

Her phone call kept going, owed to the satellites, certainly, but it was very clear the power was… Out.

Now, not only was she trapped in a snowstorm with Dario, she was trapped in a snowstorm with Dario without *power*.

And right then, it wasn't the darkness, or the potential cold that frightened her.

It was herself.

CHAPTER FOUR

"THAT CAN'T BE. He said that there was enough battery backup to last."

"Do you need me to call somebody?" Carter asked.

"I mean, maybe. You can call my dad and let him know that now we're stuck here with the power out."

"Yeah, I'll definitely do that. You should save your phone battery."

"Okay."

She hung up. Now she was standing in total darkness. And after leaving the kitchen in a huff because Dario had annoyed her, it felt absolutely irritating to stalk back in there to find him. But the problem was, she felt… Afraid.

She didn't like this at all.

She didn't want to think that she was naturally seeking out a man because she felt nervous. But the truth was, what Dario had said to her earlier had felt reassuring. He had been through a lot. He had survived a lot.

And what she tended to write off as him just being overly grand was actually a testament to all that he'd been through and all that he had accomplished.

It was easy for her to be defensive about that. Because she always felt like when he talked about his experience he was actually talking about the lack of hers.

But that was… Perhaps a limited perspective. It was perhaps selfish. Or at least self-centered.

"You said that the generator was going to work," she accused.

"Because it should," said Dario. "There was an official guide to the house and I read it."

Of course he had.

"Well, what are we going to do?"

"We're fine," he said. "We are able to have heat, and the stove is gas, so we should be able to melt snow in a pan. There's plenty of dry goods. It's hardly a difficult survival situation, and I would say at most it will only be a couple of days."

"*A couple of days*," she said.

"Yes," he said. "A couple of days. And all will be well."

"Our phones aren't going to last that long."

He lifted a brow. "Perhaps don't make video calls."

"But…"

"In fact, you should probably turn your phone off. It would be best if we made sure to conserve the battery in case we have an emergency."

"You said it wasn't an emergency. You said everything would be fine."

"I also said that the generator would work. Why are you taking everything I say as a clairvoyant prediction?"

She huffed, and looked down at her phone screen one last time. She had a text from Carter.

"Carter told my dad that the power went off."

"Excellent. I imagine he will be working to get us out of here. Text Carter and tell him you're turning your phone off to conserve battery and I'm doing the same. Tell him all is well."

She did, but put knife and gun emojis afterward, along with a skull. Then she turned the phone off.

"Do you feel better for having added drama?" Dario asked.

"Yes. Much better. A little bit of drama often makes things bearable."

"How so?"

"I just… Don't you ever feel like that? Like if you totally freak out you've sort of shown yourself the worst of it and then you can just breathe and deal with it?"

"I can't say that I do." But he almost looked like he wished he did, and that did something to her.

"I… I've never been in a situation like this before."

"You'll be just fine." He began to walk out of the kitchen.

"Where are you going?"

"Down to the basement. There's firewood down there, matches, lighters. And lanterns. I'm going to get everything that we might need to manage this."

"Oh… I don't want to go in a basement."

"Then feel free to stay up here."

He walked away, and she moved quickly after him.

"I don't want to be stuck up here without you either."

"You cannot be pleased."

"No," she said. "When snowed in with a man who

drives me insane, with absolutely no electricity, I cannot be pleased."

"Perhaps go throw yourself in a snowdrift, then."

She hissed and spit the whole way down to the basement.

"For a creature who has never lived on the streets you are quite feral," he said.

"That's very infantilizing," she said, sniffing. "I am not feral, neither am I a creature."

"Then don't act like one."

There were stacks of wood in the corner, and he moved to them, taking hold of the logs with ease.

She felt like she was meeting him for the first time and it was a bit disconcerting. She knew that Dario had grown up on the streets. But it was quite another thing to see him being so calmly capable in what could be argued was a survival situation. She saw him often as a roadblock to fling herself against. A representative of all the ways in which she didn't live up to her father's expectations. Because if she did, why would he need Dario? And in this moment, she saw him as a man. Capable. Calm in a crisis.

Exactly the sort of man she should be glad she was stuck with, and that made her feel even more annoyed, because the truth was, right now it would be better to be stuck with Dario than Carter, and she didn't even need to know what Carter's hunting and gathering skills were to know that.

Dario had legitimately spent time in survival situations. It wasn't like Boy Scout camp or watching videos on YouTube.

And if pressed, that was what she needed.

Someone who could actually guide this situation, because Lord knew she couldn't. Galling to have to admit even internally, but she wouldn't have thought to go down into the basement in the first place. She hadn't known there was a basement. She hadn't read up on the house she was staying in. Because she just expected…

She was so worried about herself right now, and about how Dario's skills were benefiting her but…he'd gotten them by suffering and that was a stark, painful realization.

"Grab some of the lanterns," he said, gesturing to a shelf that had an array of camping equipment.

She picked up a few lanterns, and also some extra blankets. Fleece and reindeer hide. Because staying cozy was very high on her list.

She followed him up the stairs carrying all of the various supplies.

"It would be best if we chose a room to make warm. I would say likely best my bedroom."

"What?" Her heart slammed against her chest.

"The living room is too open. The ceiling is high. The bedroom has a fireplace, but it is much more closed off."

"What are we… Supposed to do in there?"

As soon as she said that she regretted it. Because she felt her face and body get very hot. And she knew that she had just implanted that very same image that had been living in her head the last couple of days right into his.

He looked at her, and there was something simmering in his eyes that nearly made her heart stop. "I'm sure we'll think of something."

She was imagining that. She had to be. He was Dario Rivelli. He didn't like her. And more than that, he thought of her as a child.

The truth was, she had always seen Dario as a man. He had been a man as far as she was concerned from the first moment she had met him. It was just that his being a man didn't seem appealing to her. Until… Maybe until recently.

Liar.

All right. So there had always been tension inside of her when dealing with him. Always. And if maybe she was extra sulky when she brought him his coffee because looking at him felt uncomfortable, and made her feel awkward and like she didn't know what to do with her hands when no one and nothing else did, then… Well.

She would never have called it attraction, though.

Not until now

She had always thought of it is resentment.

But suddenly, looking at that starkly handsome face, with all the snow piled up outside and the promise of being holed up in his bedroom in front of the fireplace, she felt like she couldn't deny anymore what it was.

It wasn't an aberration that she had imagined being in the bathtub with him.

It was her true heart.

How could that be? She liked Carter. She had just talked to him on the phone and she was thrilled to hear his voice. She had imagined sitting in naked companionship with him and it had been nice. When she thought of being naked with Dario it was anything but nice. It made her feel like someone had forced a fistful of butterflies down her throat and into her stomach. It made her feel like she was being victimized by hormones.

She felt hot and cold all at once. She felt like she might be dying.

Was that how it was supposed to be?

"Lyssia," he said, the warning note in his voice doing something strange to her.

"What?"

"You know exactly what."

"I don't," she said. "I just want to know where to put the lanterns."

"My room," he said.

And that was how she found herself marching up the stairs with him. The bedroom he was staying in was large, with a huge, imposing four-poster bed in the corner.

There was a fireplace at the back wall, and because they were on the second floor, the window looked out over the mountain of snow.

She went over and peered down.

"This is... Unbelievable."

"Indeed."

He settled down in front of the fireplace and put the logs in, working at lighting the fire. He accomplished it quickly, and she could only be grateful, yet again, that she was with Dario.

Except then a moment later the realization that she was attracted to him crashed back into her. Her eyes went to his thighs. Covered by the fine wool of the pants he was wearing. He had changed since early this morning, into the regular suit pants she was used to seeing him in, and a white shirt.

The sleeves were rolled up, and she watched the play of muscles in his forearms as he moved logs into the fireplace, his motions calm and expert.

The absolute certainty in everything he did was something she had never seen in anyone else.

Dario wore excellence as a second skin.

It was something quite unlike anyone else she had ever encountered.

Many men were overconfident. Brash. Arrogant. And she would easily characterize Dario is arrogant, but the difference between him and other men was that he actually had a right to the arrogance. If he said that he could do something, then he did it. If he professed to know about something, then he did.

It made her feel safe yet again, but at the same time, she felt on edge.

What was she supposed to do with this realization that she was attracted to the man. That made her feel just a small sliver of uncertainty. Of fear.

Like she had walked into a lion's cage, and anything could happen.

His movements fluid, he moved away from the lit fire. No. He wasn't a lion. He was a panther. She didn't know why that mattered. Except in that moment, she could think of little that mattered more. Then taking in the details of him. That dark hair, black and swept off his forehead. The perfect, sculpted cheekbones and square jaw.

It was like really seeing him for the first time. She didn't want to be having this moment, and yet she was.

She was like a child. A schoolgirl. Who had been antagonizing a boy because she thought he was cute.

Except he wasn't a boy, and *cute* was an offensive term for his sophisticated looks.

She wanted to fling herself out that window right into a snowbank, as he had suggested earlier.

Except part of her was… More interested than she should be.

Is this just because you wanted to have sex this weekend?

Her stomach twisted. The hard pain more intense than anything she had felt when she had been considering sleeping with Carter.

She couldn't even fathom the fallout of sleeping with Dario.

He was always around. Brooding and dark. He was older, he was… "Is there something I can help you with?" he asked. Because of course she was staring at him, and she hadn't realized she was.

"No," she said. "Sorry."

"I have an idea. I believe there were sausages in the fridge downstairs. For now, all the things in the fridge will still be all right. But they won't be for long. We can take certain things out and shove them into the snow that's butted up against the door. And we can bring the sausages upstairs and roast them in the fire."

"Okay," she said, grateful for the break in tension.

Though sausages weren't the most nonsexual food.

The task of stuffing things into the snowbank was so amusing that she forgot for a moment that she had been awash in attraction just a few moments before. She took a jar of jam and shoved it into the snow.

"This is hilarious," she said.

"But practical," he responded. "It will keep us fed. And that way we can save the dry goods."

"True."

"How are we going to grill sausages?"

"I have an idea," he said.

He took a rack out of the oven, and a large skillet, and they went upstairs where he was able to, at great personal risk, shove the rack into the fireplace and place it on a ledge. Then he put the skillet on top and put the sausages in there.

"This is almost civilized," she said.

"Very nearly," he agreed.

They sat for a moment, regarding the food. Her stomach growled. She had that peanut butter and jelly not that long ago, but she felt like the sense that she was in a survival situation had created a bit of a psychosomatic sense that she might be starving.

Maybe she wasn't great in a crisis. She had never really thought about it one way or the other before. But now it mattered. She felt somewhat galled by the realization. That many of the things Dario had said to her over the years that felt mean were a little bit true. She had been sheltered. A little bit cosseted even, and while she had gone out on her own and done a certain number of things, she had a very large safety net. Always and ever. A big backup generator, as it were. And it had never failed her, unlike the one here.

She had felt like it did, because it had felt like her father was being unkind to her by selling the company to Dario. Which maybe wasn't fair. She didn't actually want the company. She wanted her father to…be proud.

She had tried. She had tried to be…Dario. But she wasn't.

"Is something wrong?"

His voice was dark as velvet. Just as soft. It scraped over her skin in the most deliciously uncomfortable way, and she felt like a different person, here in the silence of this house. Surrounded by snow, surrounded by him.

Normally, she would be sharp with him. Normally, she wouldn't try to see him as a person. She had seen him primarily as an obstacle, and then as an obstacle that made her feel prickly and uncomfortable as she had gotten older.

But not now. He wasn't an obstacle now. He was helping her, and unfortunately, she was also seeing new things about herself thanks to him.

It was not comfortable.

"What if I'm not as good at all of this as you and my father are? What does that say about me? And what does it say about my representation of *feminism*?"

"Who says you have to represent anything? You are not all women. You are simply you. And also, it is not about being good enough. Perhaps it is only that you are different. I couldn't design furniture. I wouldn't know where to begin."

"Well, my father doesn't esteem my ability to do that, maybe that's the problem."

He paused for a moment. "And yet what you do is esteemed, appreciated, or you wouldn't have clients."

"I don't have enough clients."

"For what?"

"For…for anyone to take me seriously." It sounded so small. But it felt so big.

"There are many people on the streets who want what I have. The truth is, I was bound and determined to make a certain thing of myself. I believe that I had advantages, even in my disadvantages. I am not a vain man, Lyssia, but I am not unaware of the fact that I'm handsome. And that I have used that as a tool. I have an easy time connecting with people, telling them exactly what they want to hear in the voice they want to hear it in. It is not a moral failure if you have not risen from the streets to have a billion dollars."

"What about rising from one billion dollars to having something of your own."

"That isn't a moral failure either."

"It feels like it."

"Your father was born rich. He built on what he had, and it is well done. You are not the same person that he is, that doesn't mean you aren't as good. It doesn't mean that you aren't successful. You're twenty-three years old. You're allowed to take some time to figure out which path you want to walk."

"There are literal chat forums on the internet about how I'm losing at the easiest setting of life."

"And what does it matter if strangers think you've failed when you haven't?"

"I… I don't know, Dario. Maybe this is the really stupid problem with having the safety net. I could never work a day in my life and I wouldn't be fighting for survival, so why am I doing it? For a feeling, I guess. For a sense that what I do matters, that my being alive matters. That I'm important and smart and… I do want people to see it. That I care. That I'm trying. And they don't. My father doesn't or he wouldn't have sent you this week. It would be me and Carter. Snowed in."

"Right."

"Having sex."

"So you say."

The silence between them lapsed. "I'm not in love with Carter. I never thought it was love or anything. But he made me feel pretty. He made me feel…"

"He made you feel good about yourself. Perhaps in part because he is not as successful as you are."

She winced. "Perhaps. That makes me sound very shallow."

"Many people cannot handle having a partner who is more successful than they are. Though, particularly, men cannot."

"Well, points for Carter, then. Because I don't think that he cared. Or maybe like everybody else he simply doesn't think I'm all that successful."

"Why have you not used your connection with your father to get more accounts?"

"I'm trying to succeed on my own."

"But that's foolishness. Nobody succeeds in business on their own. If you have connections and you don't exploit them, then what is the point? You have the advantages, and you should use them. Your real problem, Lyssia, is that you're not trying to succeed for the sake of it. You're trying to prove something. And you are doing so at the expense of yourself."

She had never thought of it that way. She thought of it as trying to be independent. "But you didn't have any connections."

"That isn't true. I started working in a kitchen with no connections, but everywhere that I worked, every customer that I came into contact with, every room that I walked into I was building connections. When you are climbing a rope up from the gutter, you realize that you need handholds. And I made handholds everywhere that I went. That is perhaps my greatest strength."

"It's different, though. When it's your father, versus..."

"It isn't. You were working with what you have, the same that I was working with what I had. I have been very hard on you," he said. "I fear that perhaps I have undermined you at certain points when I did not intend to."

Their eyes met. She found it hard just then to breathe. Her eyes suddenly stung, the pressure in her chest unbearable. She cleared her throat.

"You're not my father," she said. "So, it's not really up to you to fix all that."

He chuckled. “I know that I'm not your father.”

The air between them seemed to crackle. She decided that it was just the sausages in the pan. Because she didn't want to acknowledge that crackle. Didn't want to find herself at the mercy of it. Because it was far too much.

Or perhaps it wasn't. Perhaps it was what she needed.

No. You know you can't. Can you imagine how scathing he would be?

She wasn't sure she could withstand that level of rejection. Flinging herself at the beautiful and condescending Dario only to find herself laid low.

No. That would be an indignity too far.

“I think the food is ready,” he said, his tone mild, and she wondered if he felt the same thing that she did. She wondered if that moment had just been in her head.

He speared the sausages with a fork and put them onto a plate. Then he took out a bottle of wine and poured them each a glass. They were sitting on the floor in front of the fireplace, and it was like a picnic. It might have been romantic if he were anyone else.

She felt her face growing hot as she let that thought pass through her. As she tried to let it go.

“Thank you,” she said softly. Because she never really was all that nice to him. “I'm…quite certain that I would've panicked and run into a snowdrift without you here.”

“I don't think you would have. You're not a stupid woman. You consistently think the worst of yourself.”

She frowned. “No, I don't.”

“You do. I am realizing these past days that you do.

Why do you think you need to be with a partner who is less successful than you? Why do you think that you're a failure, when in fact you're simply young? You do not trust herself. You are the one who looks down on you."

"Also you, sometimes," she said.

"Yes. Sometimes." But there was something unreadable in his dark eyes. Like there was more that he wanted to say, but wouldn't. But didn't.

She felt tension growing in the space between them. Expanding.

She felt herself growing hot beneath the intensity of that gaze.

"Why?" she asked softly. "Why have you always been so hard on me?"

He said nothing, but regarded her closely. She felt his gaze like a physical touch, as it moved from her face, down her throat, to her breasts, down her thighs.

The open masculine appreciation nearly undid her. From Dario. Dario, who she would've said hated her. Dario, whom she would've said she hated.

But nothing that was passing between them right now felt like hatred. It felt like something much more dangerous. Something she didn't fully understand. Something she didn't have full access to. But she wanted it. It felt like something entirely different from what she had imagined she might find with Carter. But then, on some level she had known that. She had.

But… She couldn't be right about this.

"It is safer," he said finally. "To allow myself to believe that you are young. Foolish. That you do not know your own mind. And you believe that as well."

"No, I don't," she said.

"You do. It keeps you safe. In many ways, it keeps you safe."

"From?"

She knew that asking the question was dangerous. And yet, she was so close to the flame, in every way.

It made her want to reach out and touch.

In spite of it all.

She didn't move forward, but she didn't move away either. And everything in her was screaming that it would be better if she did.

But she sat, rooted to the spot. Protected, somewhat, by the way that her plate sat on top of her knees. Acting as a barrier. Sort of.

"From myself, Lyssia."

He was dangerous. That was something she knew instinctively. A truth that radiated through her. She had never been drawn to danger, not even once. She had always valued her safety. She wasn't brave. She wasn't adventurous. She wasn't…

She had chosen Carter because he represented safety. Not because she wanted him. She had told herself all kinds of stories about why she wanted something that felt easy and fun. Something that lacked intensity and consequence.

At every turn, she downplayed the deepest of her own emotions, and denied herself anything with real resonance.

Was he right? Was it because she didn't trust herself? Because she didn't pay heed to herself?

She told herself so definitively all the things that she

wanted, and in some ways, when she was telling Dario what she wanted it was like she was trying to reinforce all of those truths inside of herself.

But they started to feel thin now. For and in the face of what he had just said. That he was trying to protect her from himself.

And more than that, it was the way those words unfurled inside of her.

It was more appealing than it ought to be. And it was… Was she really understanding it right?

This was where she suddenly felt woefully inadequate next to him. He knew how to survive. He knew how to build something from nothing.

And he knew about sex. In a way that she simply didn't. It felt unbelievable that a man of his prowess would be interested in her. That he would've had to try to hold himself back from her in any capacity, and yet reading between the lines that seemed to be what he was saying.

Be brave.

"Why would I be in danger from you?"

She set her plate down. She removed the barrier.

"Lyssia…"

"Why?"

He looked pained then, as if he was on the verge of something he actually feared. And then he spoke.

"Because you are as stubborn as you are beautiful. Because you are my mentor's daughter, and far too young for me to have the thoughts that I have toward you."

Her heart jumped. Hit square against her breastbone.

"You don't like me," she whispered.

His gaze was impenetrable obsidian.

"Like and dislike have little to do with chemistry, or have you not noticed that chemistry is what we have?"

"We fight all the time."

"Why do you think that is?"

He didn't call her *child*, but she felt it was implied.

But it was also not as infuriating as it might've been. She expected it to be. It was fascinating. Like the rest of him. Like this moment. Like the fantasy that she had, unbidden, of the two of them in the tub. It had felt intrusive at the time, but now it felt… Intoxicating. It felt like it had potential. To be something. To be something that she wanted.

"I don't know. I…"

"Because you have trafficked in boys. And I am a man. As I told you, if Carter truly wanted you, then he would have spoken to you from the beginning. He would never have allowed me to take his place. He would've made alternative arrangements. You were not in the forefront of his mind. And in my opinion, when a man does not make you the beginning and end of everything, he does not deserve to have you. Why should he have access to your body? Why? If he does not make having you, cherishing you, the focus of the moment, then why give him all of you?"

"It's just that that's a very outdated—"

"Is it? Do women not surrender more during sex? Risk more?"

"I guess we do," she said. That she was unwilling to tell him that she actually didn't know firsthand.

He already thought her to be so much younger, so much less experienced, she didn't want to compound matters by letting him know just how much that was true.

"You can't possibly be saying that you're attracted to me," she said.

"Perhaps that is the problem. I am trying to say it. Perhaps it would be better if I showed you."

CHAPTER FIVE

DARIO KNEW THAT he had made a very bad deal with the devil just now. Sold a piece of his soul, and he didn't have all that many left. What he had said to Lyssia was true. He was a man who had done a very good job of making connections and then using those connections to his advantage whenever possible.

He was a man who had endured some very dark things. And he had very few connections in this world that were not about business. Her father was one of them. She was the other.

For that reason alone she had always been sacred to him. The connection had been sacred. They were fire and flame, and honesty—except in this. And now he had done it. He'd forced this truth into the open between them. And here they were, in the snow, the power out. And somehow, he had taken that connection and twisted inside of himself. He was telling himself now that she needed to know. That she needed to know what it was like to be with a man.

A man who wanted her.

A man who would not give her insipid sex and a

wishy-washy petering out, or worse still, a ghosting. Dario was definitive.

No, he could not give her a relationship, but he would give her honesty. He would give her good sex, and worship her the way she should be.

She needed to know what it was to have her body cherished. Lavished with pleasure.

And that, that rationalization, that was straight from Satan himself. But it was not the first deal that Dario had made with the dark Lord, and wouldn't be the last. And so, he found himself moving toward her, cupping the back of her head and bringing her in to kiss her mouth.

The sound she made was shocked and short.

And for a moment, she was still beneath his mouth, but then, she surrendered. Like a flower beginning to open. Her lips softened, parted, and when he slid his tongue against hers she responded in kind.

Suddenly, her hand came up to grip his shoulders, and she was moving toward him, leaning against him, her whole body pressed to his.

She was behaving as if she had never experienced anything like this before, and he knew that he hadn't.

The softness of her mouth, the sweetness of it, was a sucker punch. It was beyond. He always liked women, but he had known from the moment he had begun to feel attraction for Lyssia that the real danger with her was a chemistry that existed between them that she wasn't even aware of. Her whimper was one of helplessness, and as she clung to him, her kiss became bolder.

And that was when he moved. He pressed her down to the floor in front of the fireplace, licking his way into her mouth as he gave himself over to the clawing need between them.

It had always been this. Burning between them. What he had attempted to handle with indifference could no longer be contained, because he could not find a shred of indifference left in his soul.

He was jaded.

And from the beginning, the way that he felt for Lyssia challenged that jadedness.

It was dangerous.

It always had been.

He heard stories about such things, and he had always doubted them. That there was the potential for chemistry to overwhelm everything. Good sense and the whole of a man's nature.

He had never believed it. He had always thought that it was an excuse for weakness. Perhaps this was weakness now.

No. It was not a weakness. He had made a decision. He had made a bargain. And he had followed through with it.

It was no less than he did with a business deal. With anything. They were here, they were snowed in. It was an opportunity. A connection. And it had to be managed.

And managed it would be.

He stripped her sweatshirt from her body, followed by her shirt. She had a fine, white lace bra underneath that showed the pale shadow of her nipples.

She was beautiful.

So far beyond anything he had imagined she might be.

Beneath the cups of the bra was a delicate gold chain, linked in lovely intervals to the delicate fabric, creating a seductive design.

"What is this?" he asked, moving his thumb across one of the gold chains.

"It's… I had… I mean, you saw my suitcase," she said, breathless.

"Yes. I did. Was this for you to seduce him?"

"Yes. But obviously, I thought that maybe I would wear it because…"

"Were you going to seduce me, Lyssia?"

She laughed. "No. I wasn't that brave."

He looked down at her face, those glorious, glittering blue eyes. "Why do you not think you're brave?"

"I'm not. I…"

He gripped her chin and held her gaze. "You are brave. You have not been put to the test, but that does not mean that you aren't brave. I know you feel as if you were not strong today, but if you were by yourself, you would have done well. You would have figured it out. Let me show you how brave you are."

He knew this because of her spirit. He knew this because she tested him, tried him. He knew because she was Lyssia. And that had been all-consuming for quite some time.

He kissed her again, capturing her beautiful pink mouth and plunging his tongue deep. She gasped, arching against him. Her delicate hands moved over his shoulders, down his back. He growled and flexed his hips against her.

She moaned, unable to keep herself from trembling. She wanted him. As much as he wanted her.

"Did you want to seduce me?" he asked.

She looked down. "I was… I was beginning to come around to the idea."

"Look at me," he said. She obeyed, her blue eyes meeting his. "Tell me," he growled, as he kissed his way down her neck, over the plump, delicate curve of her breasts and down her stomach.

He gripped the waistband of her soft, cashmere sweatpants and dragged them down her legs, revealing a matching pair of underwear beneath. Lace and see-through with a keyhole just above the most intimate part of her, a gold chain creating a delicate web there.

"Tell me," he commanded.

"I… When I got here, I looked at the tub, and I imagined being in the tub with you. And it shook me, because I… I have pretended all this time that what I feel for you is nothing short of animosity. Because it's easier. It's so much easier. Because there's no point in having a wild, sexual need for a much older man, is there? Especially when he just thinks that you're a silly girl."

"I don't think you're a silly girl," he said. He moved his fingertips beneath the waistband of her panties. "You are beautiful. And you are smart, and you are brave. And you will find your way."

"Is this a motivational speech or are we about to have sex?"

There was Lyssia. Dry and spiky as ever. And of course when she put it like that, in such bland terminology, he knew that it should make him want to pull away from her, but he found that he didn't. He just didn't. He had made his devil's bargain. His mind was made up.

"Oh, we're going to have sex," he said. "You have no idea how long I've waited for this."

Her cheeks turned pink. "You have?"

"You are a problem," he ground out. "One that I have done my best not to take in hand. To not solve the way that I wanted to. Because I knew it would create only difficulty for me. If your father were to find out..."

"He would kill you."

"Very likely."

"He doesn't have to find out."

"No. He doesn't. You should know what it feels like when a man wants you. When he really wants you."

He took her delicate hand and guided it to the front of his pants. He let her feel him. How hard he was.

Her eyes went wide. She caressed him, slowly and deliberately through the fabric of the pants.

"What are you thinking?" he asked as he watched her breathing increase, as he watched her eyes go wide.

"Well, you are rather substantial."

He chuckled. "I do well enough."

"That is the kind of thing that men who are well endowed say. Because men who are not well endowed cannot joke about... Such things."

"The voice of experience?"

"I have been in the world."

"The world is often a disappointing place," he said. "But I will endeavor to not disappoint."

"I'm not concerned," she said, her breathing becoming ragged.

He pushed his hand down the rest of the way, into her panties, between her legs. He found her slick there, hot and clearly needy.

She gasped, arching her hips upward, and he began to stroke her slowly.

He watched her face, that beautiful, familiar face, flushed with pleasure.

He did not often make love to women he knew. In fact, he didn't think he ever had.

Yes, he had associations with women that lasted through multiple trysts, but he never got to know the woman. He knew Lyssia. He knew where she came from. He knew how she had grown up. He'd been in her childhood home. He had watched her grow from a quiet child to a sulky teenager, to a beautiful woman.

He knew her.

He knew her father, he respected her father. He knew that if her father were to find out about this that… It would compromise the only real relationship that he had in his life, and here he was.

This was sweeter for knowing her. And he would never have said that that was the case when it came to sex, but now it was.

He stroked her, and she removed her hand from him, clenching those fingers into fists and letting her head fall back as she continued to roll her hips in time with the movement.

"Do you like my touch?" he asked.

"Yes," she panted.

"What do you want?"

"You," she said.

"Be brave," he ground out.

He was poised on the brink of destruction. Past his own breaking point, for if he had not broken he wouldn't be here. He would not have sold himself for this.

But what a prize. Worth the cost.

He could think of nothing but this. Of how much he wanted her.

There was nothing outside this space. No consequence, nothing.

"You inside of me," she panted. "Please. *Please.*"

He growled, pushing a finger deep inside of her, and she moaned with pleasure, throwing her forearm over her eyes as the beginnings of an orgasm began to ripple through her.

He pushed a second finger inside her and pushed her over the edge. She gasped, then cried out, biting her lip, her eyes still covered by her forearm.

"Dario," she whispered.

"Yes," he ground out.

And when she shattered, it was complete. When she shattered, he felt himself lose his tether on his control.

He wanted Lyssia Anderson, and he was going to have her.

CHAPTER SIX

LYSSIA COULDN'T BELIEVE this was happening. She couldn't believe that Dario had just touched her to orgasm, that she had demanded he do so.

What was wrong with her?

She didn't know herself. Or perhaps what was worse was she did. She felt like there had been a great veil ripped away. She felt like all of the lies that she had told herself for all of this time had been burned to the ground. Sizzled over an open flame like a bunch of emergency sausages.

She was at sea.

Or perhaps just buried in a snowdrift.

She wanted him. She was certain of that. And as she looked into his blazing, dark eyes she knew with absolute certainty that she had wanted him all this time.

That the edge beneath her skin when she looked at him was desire.

But the absolute pull of need that wound its way through her like a live wire was deeper and more consequential than she would have ever wanted to admit.

It was not simple aesthetic appreciation for his perfectly formed features. It was not just an acknowledgment that he was a handsome enough man.

No. She wanted him.

Every time she had been tempted to misbehave to get his attention when she had been his assistant, every time she had snapped at him rather than being civil or sane.

When she had come here and he had arrived, she hadn't been angry that he was here. She was angry because what she wanted was to want another man, and she simply didn't. Simply couldn't.

Not in the way that she wanted him. Being irritated with Dario Rivelli was more exciting than being attracted to Carter had ever been, and now that she saw it through this perfect lens, she knew that it had always been need.

She had been angry about it.

She had been resentful of it, but it was very much the truth. She wanted him.

Oh, how she wanted him.

"Make love to me," she whispered, wondering who belonged to that husky voice that had come out of her mouth.

She felt like an entirely different creature. But she wanted to be brave.

He had told her that she was, and now she wanted to rise to the occasion. She wanted to demand all the things she wanted, she just needed to know what they were. It wasn't that she was totally innocent, it was just that when she had imagined being with somebody finally, she hadn't really imagined it in a detailed way.

She hadn't really imagined it in a graphic way. And she could already tell that this was going to be rawer, more physical than she had given space for it to be.

She had never been a raw or physical person. She had not been especially brave in her life.

She had been hampered by a desire to please. Oh, how she had wanted to make her father proud. She wanted to be acceptable. Not good, because it wasn't like she was a robot. She had been sulky as an assistant. She had not been perfect.

She had not been enough, trying to live in the space where she could fill the hold her mother had left. Fearing the world, knowing how fragile life was, grieving and stagnating while trying to push forward and heal.

She had wanted to carve out a system of success for herself, but she had been afraid to push too far out because what she really wanted was to be wholly approved of.

She wasn't sure that was possible. But she had tried.

Oh, she had tried.

But this wasn't about pleasing anybody. Not anybody but herself. She wanted him. And she was going to have him.

Outside of this room it wouldn't make any sense. Outside of this moment. It would be desire as a spark, and nothing more. But here, it raged. Here it became an unstoppable force. A wildfire.

And she was happy to let it burn.

Nobody else ever had to know. It could just be a secret between them. Just tonight. Just this moment.

That made her feel alive. Invigorated. If this was her

night with Dario, the one and only night ever, then she could be whoever she wanted to be. And when they were free of this place they would go back to being the way they had been. He was experienced. It would mean nothing overly significant to him. And she was realistic.

"Take your clothes off," she commanded.

He arched a dark brow. "Giving orders?"

"I want to see you," she said.

"Do you?"

"Yes. You're beautiful. The most beautiful man that I've ever seen. And I have found that confronting all this time. You're right. I did want control."

"And now you'll surrender it," he said. "I don't think I'll take my clothes off. Not now. Now, I think you have to wait. But I think you will get naked for me."

His high-handed tone should irritate her, but instead she felt herself growing even wetter with her need for him. She'd already had an orgasm, but she could feel another one building. He wasn't even touching her, it was just because of the way he was looking at her. And suddenly, her body felt more beautiful than it ever had. Felt powerful. Because she could see the need in his eyes, the need to see her. The need to touch her.

She moved into a sitting position, reached behind herself and took off her bra. The chains made a soft sound as she flung it to the floor. She watched as his gaze fell to her breasts, and then she stood up, pushing her underwear down her legs, all the way to the floor, stepping out of them. "Is this what you had in mind?"

He got up on his knees and growled. Then he cupped

her ass with his hands, and brought her forward, taking a long, slow stroke of the cleft between her thighs, tasting her like she was ice cream.

She let out a shocked sound, forking her fingers into his hair as she widened her stance so that he could have greater access to the most intimate part of her.

He stroked her, the witness there easing his passage.

She was almost embarrassed by it, but... This was her night.

So instead she held his face there, moving her hips in time with the stroke from his tongue.

"Come," he commanded.

"I just did," she panted.

"Come again," he growled, his teeth scraping against her sensitive skin before he slicked his tongue over her body one more time and she came apart.

She shuddered and shattered, her whole world reduced to sparkling shards.

She was remade beneath that mouth. That beautiful, glorious mouth.

If she had the potential to be shocked by it, it wasn't here. Not in this moment.

"Dario," she whispered.

He rose to his feet and picked her up off the ground, moving his hands down her thighs and lifting her and encouraging her to put her legs around his waist.

She moaned, and he laid her down on his bed, rising up over her, and leaning down to kiss her mouth. She could taste her own desire there, the force of her own need.

She felt like perhaps that should embarrass her also.

But there just was no embarrassment here. There was nothing but want. Nothing but need.

It was cascading glory, and she wanted to capture each and every glimmer.

He moved away from her, and stripped his shirt up over his head, revealing his glorious body. His dark, heavily muscled chest with dark hair sprinkled across. She watched the shift and bunch of his muscles, the glory of his abs.

Then he pushed his sweats and underwear down his legs, leaving him entirely exposed to her gaze. She had never seen a naked man in person before.

He was... He was incredible. Just beautiful.

If they wanted to make a real, impressive classical statue, then Dario would be the perfect model.

But he would leave all those other Italian sculptures shamed in his wake.

"I'm on the pill," she blurted out.

She took a low-dose birth control pill to help with her periods. And she had thought that it was probably a handy thing, for when she did become sexually active. And, she had always intended to use it in conjunction with condoms, since that was responsible. But she was stuck in a house with Dario, and she imagined he hadn't brought any. She was not about to let that disrupt the moment.

"Good," he said, short and sharp.

He moved back to the bed, back to her, kissing her deeply, pressed against her body, the heat of his skin, all that bare skin, leaving her breathless.

"Dario," she whispered.

"Beautiful," he said against her mouth. *"Bellissima."*

She shivered. She would've told anyone who asked that she wasn't the kind of woman to get silly over accents and foreign endearments, but here she was. Melting.

He gripped her thigh and hooked it up over his narrow hip, moved his hardness through her slick folds, ramping up her desire.

She'd already come twice, but this was… Waiting was killing her. She needed him. Needed to know what it was like to be filled by him. She ached. She felt hollow with her need for him.

His name was a drumbeat on her lips, a rhythm in her soul.

And finally, he pressed himself to the entrance of her body, and pushed home.

She gripped his shoulders. "Ouch!"

"Lyssia?"

A litany of curses went through her head and she tried to collect herself. She hadn't expected it to *hurt.* Not *really.*

She hadn't had anyone to talk to deeply about this and everyone around her acted like sex just wasn't a big deal, and so she'd imagined it must not be.

"I thought hymens were a societal construct," she said, trying to deny the pain and the rising tide of emotion inside her.

"What?"

"It's just that… I thought that virginity was a completely social construct and the myth of the hymen was…"

He started to withdraw from her and she put her hands on his shoulder. "Don't," she said.

"You're not telling me that you were a virgin," he said fiercely.

"I guess so, but I didn't really ever think of it—" except when she did "—because, you know, that's all patriarchal nonsense designed to scare women. To control them. I didn't really think that it hurt the first time."

"Did you think women were lying to you?" He had never even been with a virgin and he knew that it hurt the first time.

"I didn't think they were lying, I just thought that… I don't know…the idea was implanted there ahead by the patriarchy, and then…"

"If you had told me I would have eased the way."

"You kind of tried to do that. But you… You're substantial."

"If you're a virgin, how would you even know?"

"It's not like I've never seen a naked man. On the computer."

"Lyssia," he said. "You cannot tell me that I just deflowered you."

She sniffed and tried to play unbothered. With him over her. In her. Talking to her. "I won't, because that is a vile term."

She was trying to be cool, but in reality she felt panicky, and upset. Because she didn't want that to be her only experience of sex. She wanted *him*.

But it had hurt and she hadn't been able to hold back. She had no defenses. Nothing. It felt like being hit, square on by life, except she'd jumped into this feet-first.

He started to move away from her again and this time, she gripped him more gently. But more urgently. "Please don't leave me," she said.

"Lyssia… I won't."

"I just need a minute."

She acclimated to the feel of him. Hard and pulsing inside of her. It was different. Different from anything she'd ever experienced before.

It felt good. Amazing even. But it was definitely not what she'd anticipated.

And then, as the pain slowly subsided, desire began to return. And he began to move. So deep inside of her, and she realized that it wasn't what she had expected in many, many ways.

She had thought that she would have some control over this. She thought that she would be able to have sex and walk away without an emotional connection.

But it wasn't what she was experiencing. Not now. Not with him.

Not with him, she said to herself.

Because she couldn't be feeling this for him.

But then, his strokes turned from pain all the way to pleasure, and she could no longer think. She could only feel. That deep need within her driving her now. Urging her on.

She moaned as he thrust inside of her, as her internal muscles gripped him tight.

He held her hips, looking into her eyes as he built need within her with every movement of his body within hers.

She answered each thrust in kind, and when her climax broke over her, he gave himself up to it as well, on a growl, and she felt him pulse deep within her.

She clung to him, shuttering as wave after wave of need overtook her.

As he poured himself inside of her.

And when it was done, she clung to his shoulders. And she didn't cry, only because she couldn't. Because she couldn't let her guard down quite so much. Because she couldn't admit that it had been quite so intense.

"You should've told me," he said.

It hurt that he was being so curt and cold now. But she shouldn't be needy. She shouldn't be looking for affirmations.

She'd been so sure she'd be okay with this. That it wouldn't matter. Because she knew better than to be needy. She knew that you couldn't count on life to not pull the rug out from under you.

But she felt needy for him. And she knew she shouldn't. She'd wanted sex to be a nice thing she could have. Something that made her feel special or cherished, maybe even the most of something. To someone like Carter, even. It had seemed possible.

She hadn't wanted to be torn asunder by it emotionally. Hadn't wanted to feel scorched.

She'd been a little girl when her mother had died, so of course she'd depended on her mother, and the loss had been crippling.

She knew better now, though.

Knew better than to want to cling to a man who'd only had sex with her.

Because sex was nothing really all that deep, was it?

"Well, I didn't," she said. "I didn't think that it mattered. I didn't think it was your business. Also, I didn't know that you would assume anything about my sexual status."

"You were ready to seduce Carter. That was how you were going to lose your virginity?"

"Virginity doesn't mean anything," she said, ignoring her throat going tight. "Please don't yell at me. We just… We've just been together and I can't… I can't…"

And suddenly, his strong arms went around her, and she wanted to stop with relief. She buried her head in his bare chest, her palms pressed against his muscles. She relished the feel of his chest hair. The feel of his body against hers.

"I'm sorry," he said. "I did not mean to be harsh with you. But you must know that I…"

"I know," she said. "It's just for this. Just for now. We are snowed in together, so let's just… Be together for this. Only for this."

"It could be tonight. It could be tomorrow."

"I know," she said softly. "I know that's all it might be. I'm okay with that."

She wasn't sure what she was okay with. She didn't feel okay now at all. She wasn't sure why she was speaking with such authority when she wasn't entirely sure there was a name for the emotions that were rioting through her.

Maybe because she needed to believe it herself, far more than she needed him to believe it.

"All right. If that's what you want."

"It's what I want."

"Then that's what shall be."

She could have made fun of him. For acting like having sex with her was such a big, arduous task. But she felt far too raw.

They slept on the same bed but didn't cuddle. But then, he reached over and found her, and took her again. And after that, he held her.

After that, they didn't talk about her past experience—or lack of it. They didn't talk about anything. They also didn't wear clothes. They stayed in his room unless they had to go forage for food. They made love, and they slept. For three days. It was all there was. There was no world beyond Lyssia and Dario.

She forgot why it was improbable. She forgot why they were unlikely. She could barely remember a time when she hadn't known Dario's body.

She couldn't imagine going back.

She couldn't.

But on the third day, Dario came back to his bedroom wearing sweatpants, looking grim.

"Your father has just arrived. Or rather, he is about to. The helicopter has landed out the front.

"Oh."

"Get dressed," he said, sharp and curt.

And she obeyed, because what else was there to do.

She looked out the window, and saw not just her father, but a snowplow. Along with a team of people. And that was when the attempt to free them began in earnest. It took several hours, and the entire time, she sat there with Dario, not speaking, not touching. By the time the door opened and her father appeared, the mask that Dario wore was so convincing that even she wouldn't have guessed at everything behind it.

Even she would never have known that they had ever been lovers.

He was as he'd ever been.

And she tried to be too.

"I'm so glad you survived," her father said, half joking, she could tell by his tone. But not entirely.

"And then, they were whisked outside, and to the helicopter. And when they left that cocoon, she knew that they would never be able to go back.

And part of her broke in half.

CHAPTER SEVEN

In the six weeks since they'd returned from being snowed in, Dario hadn't seen Lyssia at all. She had been completely scarce around the office, and she hadn't contacted him.

He didn't know why she would have.

He was the one that had made it clear that they needed to keep what was between them at the chalet. But he thought about her. All the time. He woke up having dreamed about her.

He had no interest in other women. It was grim and unprecedented. And it was beginning to affect his work.

But he felt like something had changed within him, and so it all felt… Wrong.

He did not like things to feel wrong, and he did not like marinating in feelings. He didn't like feelings at all.

He opened up his computer and saw he had an email. He clicked on it, and saw that it was a newsletter from Anderson Group, and announcing a partnership with Lyssia's brand.

"Well, it's about time," he said.

He knew that she had resisted that. But it was good business, and it was going to save her interiors company.

He thought, for a moment, that it might be because of the time they had spent together. He wanted to believe it was.

Why is that? It doesn't matter if you affected her in some way.

His phone rang then, and he answered it.

"Mr. Rivelli, Lyssia Anderson's office called. She has requested an appointment with you in the morning."

"I'm busy," he said, the words as a reflex when they tumbled from his mouth.

"She thought you might say that, but she said she has an offer to make you, and also some information."

"Information?" He was trying to imagine what Lyssia could possibly have to tell him.

"I have meetings."

"She knew that you would say that. She wondered if there was any possible way that you could take a drop-in now."

"Now?"

"She's at the front desk."

He had a meeting at ten minutes. He was going to cancel it. Because Lyssia was here, and he wanted to know what she was going to tell him.

He looked back at the email with the announcement. He had a feeling it was to do with her business. Perhaps she was going to try to get him to use her interiors in his properties. It would be the smart thing for her to do.

So yes. He would see her. It would be good. For both of them, perhaps. A unifying theme throughout the resorts, since Anderson was on the cusp of becoming his.

"Yes," he said. "Move my three thirty and send her in."

He sat down behind his desk and looked at the room.

It was large, with windows that overlooked the city below. He had always loved that view. Especially of Central Park in the fall. When the colors shifted

Coming to New York for the first time had felt like stepping into another life. It had been.

He had been overawed by the place. And he had felt small in it. Gazing up at the buildings.

Now he gazed down at them from a building of his own.

What would Lyssia say when she came in?

It was the last thought he had before the door to the office opened.

He felt like his heart was going to burst through his chest when he saw her. She looked amazing. Her blond hair was pulled back into a low bun, her curves highlighted beautifully by the white sheath dress she wore.

There was a delicate golden locket hanging around her neck. And her shoes were bright pink.

She looked like a more polished version of herself. And just as glorious.

"Thank you for seeing me the last minute," she said. She had a folder held to her chest, and he nearly laughed at the way she was addressing him. Cold and professional. When only weeks ago he'd had her naked and undone in his bed.

"Of course. You know you don't need a business meeting to see me."

"This is business. I have two important matters to discuss with you. I assume you saw the announcement about Anderson."

"Yes. I assume that explains your timing."

She nodded. "Correct. I worked with my father on the press release. I knew exactly when it was going to go out."

"Very good," he said. "What triggered all this?"

"Me," she said. "I asked for what I wanted."

He did feel proud of her then. Because this was a different side of her. This was the side he always knew was there.

She was bright-eyed and eager. He had seen flashes of this. It was part of that sulky behavior, but this was it channeled. Directed.

"I want for us to work together. I would like for your resorts to consider carrying my line of home goods. We are expanding. Now that I have the contract with Anderson, I can afford to move into larger furnishings. I have several options that I think will suit the aesthetic of your chain. And we are willing to make certain things exclusive to the Rivelli brand."

"I assume that they are made from recycled materials?"

"You'll find the information on the carbon footprint in the paperwork. I think that you will be happy with it."

She shoved one folder at him.

He took it, and began to leaf through it. "I will need some time to..."

"That's fine. But while you consider that, there is one more thing that I need to speak to you about."

"And that is?"

"A custody agreement. You see, I'm pregnant, and I know that it's your baby. So we need to figure out the logistics of that deal as well."

CHAPTER EIGHT

She was so proud of herself for not breaking into pieces the moment the words left her mouth. It was a challenge. More than a challenge.

But she had fantastic high heels and a plan.

What could go wrong?

She had rehearsed this in the mirror. She had spent hours putting her outfit together. She had been relatively unstable for the last several days. After her time with Dario had ended, she had gone home and decided to figure out what she was going to do with her business. She had thought a lot about what he said. About her bravery. And about her needing to use her connections. All good. And she had been feeling really confident about it. She had talked to her dad. It had been easier than she'd imagined it might be.

He was hesitant about a few things, but they weren't unreasonable. She could see he actually did respect her ideas. She'd been afraid he didn't. Like, very profoundly afraid. And when she'd actually spoken to him and he'd been open to it, it had been like a huge sigh of relief.

And then her period hadn't come. And that had been a worry.

Because the thing was, she'd never had sex before. So when your normally regular period took a vacation in the weeks following your first intercourse, it was a real concern.

It hadn't come. And it hadn't come. So then she took a pregnancy test. And she was pregnant.

She had called her doctor and had some words with her about that birth control pill.

The issue with low-dose pills, her doctor had told her, was that for some women they were less effective.

She had thrown her phone across the room. And thrown her pills in the trash. One by one for special effect.

She had considered all her options.

And then she had…

She had sat down in her room and looked at the framed photo she kept of her mother.

She could barely remember the way that her mother's voice had sounded now. She remembered her hands. She remembered how soft they were. How it had felt when she touched her.

She remembered that she had felt so loved. So cherished always.

And then she was gone.

That was when Lyssia had known that she was going to have the baby. Because that ghost of a memory was the most real thing she had ever experienced, and she wanted that. She wanted a child to love. She wanted to be a mother. And yes, there were going to be…

Some issues. She was going to have to tell Dario. She was going to have to tell her father. She had decided that she could handle it. She had just made a very real business plan, and she had decided to attack custody the same way.

And so now here she was. It seemed a lot more reasonable in its inception. Now it seemed a little bit over the top.

"Lyssia…" He was speechless. She had rendered *Dario* speechless.

It had been a pretty shocking time for her, so it seemed fair.

"I didn't quite know the best way to tell you, but I thought that it would be best to speak when I had everything planned. So this is my proposal for custody…"

"Custody?" he asked, his voice dripping with disdain.

"Yes. Custody."

Above all else, as she had sat in that dark room and thought about her child. She had realized that she wanted her child to be proud of her. If she was going to share custody with Dario that meant that when the child was with their father, they would only be with him. When they were with her, they would only be with her. And she didn't want a child going from their wonderful, accomplished, type A father to a mother who wasn't as successful.

And that was when she had decided that she was going to get a contract with Dario's company too. Because she wanted her child to be able to be proud of her.

It felt important. And that was holding her steady now. She wanted to be admirable. And this, she felt, was admirable. She was facing everything head-on, she was being mature and adult. She was owning her responsibilities.

"Yes," she said again. "*Custody*. Because of course we need to make sure that we have an amicable arrangement in place..."

"As if we will be... Co-parenting?"

"Yes," she said. "What else would we do? Unless... If you don't want to be part of the child's life, that is okay. I'm fully prepared to—"

"Absolutely not," he said. "Under no circumstances will any child of mine be abandoned by the father. And under no circumstances will any child of mine not live in my household. You will marry me, Lyssia."

She stood there, staring at him. And then, he was standing, and she had to look up, quite a bit up, to make eye contact with him. She was thankful the desk was between them because the impact of him was overwhelming. The memory of that night over a month ago was burned into her.

She would've thought that being with him like that might have demystified him. That she would feel... If not ambivalent, then at least like it was all settled. But instead, she felt like she was dangerously close to an electrical wire when she looked at him.

Like she was in danger of being shocked. And worse, like she might want to be.

She was trying to keep her guard up. Trying to keep herself from crumbling.

"We don't need to marry," she said.

"I do not want my child growing up in a broken home."

"My home was broken," she said. "It wasn't my mother's fault that she died. Our child will have both parents. That isn't a bad thing. And we've known each other for years. Surely we can be civil."

"We can be, but I won't be. I want to have our child living with married parents under one roof."

"Why?" she asked, feeling all of her control slipping.

She just couldn't handle this.

She had come to a place where she thought that she could do this. If anything, she had been worried that he wouldn't want the child. It had never occurred to her that he would demand that she marry him.

How could she…

How could she marry him? They weren't in a relationship. And she was just starting out with her business, and she was getting used to the idea of using her connections. But to be her father's daughter, and Dario's wife…

He's the father of your child either way. It isn't like you're going to get rid of your connection to him.

She gritted her teeth. Maybe. But he didn't love her. And she was definitely not in a position where she wanted to be tied to a man who could not fall in love with her. She'd never seen Dario have a relationship that lasted longer than a photo op.

She just had sex for the first time. There had to be

more out there. She didn't know what sort of man she wanted. She didn't…

"That's ridiculous," she said.

"Why? What better reason to marry than a child?"

"Love?"

"Love is a fantasy. And some people do a very admirable job of getting lost in it. But those of us who live as I did don't have the luxury. And when you do not have that luxury you cannot buy into anything beyond what you can see and feel and touch."

"Dario…"

"I told you I lived on the streets. Everyone knows this."

"Yes, you did."

"But do you know how I got there?"

She shook her head. "No. How would I know unless you told me?"

"Then now I'll tell you. After my mother died he could no longer afford me. And he sold me. He sold me to a family who used me as manual labor, and believe me, I know that I did better than I might have. There are much worse uses people find for children. Instead, I was only expected to do hard labor. But that was how much my father loved me. I will not have any child of mine experience any potential instability."

It was like the room had been stripped of the ceiling, like the sky above was howling like a wolf.

Sold?

That boy she'd seen in her mind, sleeping on the streets, was suddenly right there again. Suddenly with her. And it was like everything was…pain. It was difficult for her to fully wrap her mind around what he had just said. She had conflicts with her father, and she had certainly let herself wallow in this idea that he might not love her quite as much as perhaps her mother had, or as much as he did Dario. But her father had never left her unsafe. And he would never have done anything like that. She knew in that moment, that if her father had been faced with abject poverty when her mother had died he would've taken care of her. Without question. He would have sacrificed it all for her.

And Dario…

He'd told her it was the usual sad story and it wasn't. There was nothing usual about this. It was barbaric and horrible and beyond imagination.

"I don't know what to say," she said. "It's horrible, it's awful, it's…"

"You can see why I insist on marriage."

"No. I don't. I don't understand why you think we need to be married in order to have these kinds of supports and stability in place. We can have a custody arrangement. We… We are in each other's lives, Dario, it isn't like we can't figure out a way to share a child. Nothing bad has happened between us."

"It isn't acceptable," he said. "I would give a child of mine everything."

"I didn't think you wanted children. Ever. As you are Dario Rivelli and if you wanted something you'd have had it by now."

"I didn't. But you are having one. And it is mine. There will be no other man raising my child. Did you harbor fantasies about that? Did you think perhaps you could convince golden retriever Carter to take on that role?"

"No," she said. "No. I didn't. I wouldn't. Ever. I came to you as soon as I figured out what I wanted to do. I came to you as soon as I had a plan. I'm doing what you said. I'm taking control. I'm not afraid. I think that this is the best—"

"You're wrong. The best thing for our child, the best thing for all of us would be if we were a family unit."

"What does that look like to you?"

"We will be married. Our child will not be subjected to censure. Think about it. Think about the sorts of articles that will be written about you and I if it does not look like we are in a real relationship."

"So that's what you're worried about. You know no one cares anymore if people are married."

"It is the principle. We do not wish to invite speculation. We will marry. It certainly doesn't matter if it's clear you were pregnant prior to the marriage, but there is no need for people to wonder or guess at the nature of our relationship."

"You would rather sell a lie."

"You're damn right I would. Instead of having… Online lists written about deadbeat billionaire father's or whatever else."

"I wasn't under the impression that you cared about that kind of thing," she said.

"I care about it in regard to my child. I will never give my child reason to doubt my care. My…my willingness to be there for them. I will never."

"I think that you're being—"

"Perhaps," he said. "But if we do this wrong we cannot go back and make it right. If we do this wrong, then we cannot go back and redo it. What is out there will be out there for all the world."

"I think the solution to that is to communicate with our child," she said.

"You want something from me, Lyssia. You want a business deal. Fine. Marry me, and it's yours."

"Are you kidding me? That is the most sexist, archaic thing that I have ever heard. I have to marry you in order to get a business deal. And it isn't going to be based on merit in any fashion."

"Did you think that it would be? You came in here with a business plan, yes, but you also came in bound and determined to tell me exactly how it was going to be with our child. Did you think that you were going to announce you are having my baby and then my decision as to whether or not I was going to go into business with you would be neutral?"

Well, she'd thought he was reasonable, and a businessman first. Every time she'd tried to bring up the subject of her issues with her father he'd been very black-and-white about all of it. If she was cared for, why was she mad? Like the finer emotional points didn't matter.

Given what she now knew about his childhood, she could understand that.

But still, she had expected him to take a cool approach to the idea of fatherhood. To be…appropriate, yes, but to want the bare minimum.

"I don't know," she said. "I don't know how to reach

you. It never occurred to me that you would want to marry me. It never occurred to me that emotion would come into a business deal at all for you."

"You have never known me. I am not a cold man. I..."

He seemed at a loss for words, and that was an unusual thing. But did he really think he wasn't cold? He hadn't been during their time together, but then he'd cut her off like nothing had happened.

So yes, he could burn blazing hot, but he could definitely be cold. And his being filled with umbrage about it was a bit much for her.

"You acted as if nothing happened between us. When my father came to the house, it was like you were a stranger again." It made her vulnerable to admit that, but he had to know. They'd always had honesty between them. Even if it was easier to play with verbal knives before they'd become lovers. And now she felt wretched and upset but she wasn't going to lie.

"What exactly did you wish me to do? Did you wish me to lay you down across the rug as our rescuers descended upon us and give them an example of how we had spent the last days?"

"I don't know. I wanted something. You never reach out to me."

"And neither did you."

"Why would I?" she asked. "It did not feel to me like there was any reason to. You were the one that said you couldn't offer me anything. And now you're insisting on marriage."

"I can't offer you what you want."

"What did you think I wanted?"

"Most women want love," he said, his tone flat.

She made a show of looking around the office, a hand pressed to her forehead as if she was blocking out the sun to look far and wide.

"What are you doing?" he asked.

"Looking for all the women you've no doubt slept with, to see if they're loitering around wishing for love."

"Of course they are not here."

"So clearly they didn't need love. What makes you think I do? I might not want a marriage destined to be loveless, but I never said I was sitting around waiting for you to love me."

"In an ideal world I would not demand marriage of you, because I would hate to make you miserable."

"But you'll make me miserable for what you consider to be the sake of our child?"

"Yes. I will. There will be time enough to discuss logistics later. I am not suggesting that we live a traditional marriage for the entire life of our child. But I am suggesting that I want it as a foundation. I am not suggesting, I am demanding. And I will not be denied."

"And if I say no?"

"I cannot force you. But I would hope that you'd see reason. And I would hope that this business deal would be enough enticement."

"If it isn't, am I to expect threats?"

"No. There is no reason to issue threats. I'm correct. I think with time you'll realize that, but I do feel that it would be better if you would come to that conclusion quickly. You expect that we are to go to your father and tell him that you are having my baby and that you aren't going to marry me?"

"Is that your real concern? That my father will be angry at you?"

"It is a concern."

And he was Dario's family. She did understand that. But also, they were supposed to be something to each other and what he was proposing just seemed…outlandish.

"What does family mean to you?"

"Why do you need to know this?"

"I feel like I can't possibly marry you or even enter into a discussion until I know what it means. What is love to you, and what will you give to our child?"

He looked at her, his dark eyes intense. And she could see that he didn't want to be questioned. It was too bad. Because she was going to question him. She was going to question this.

It was fair. Because…

She wanted to know what she was potentially signing herself up for. It was only fair.

"Family is what your father has done for you," he said finally. "It is taking care of one another. It is the only place I have ever seen it. My own family did not treat love as if it was unconditional. What I know more than anything is what I don't want. And what I will not allow."

"And what about giving more than material wealth to your child?"

"I want to make a family, does that not demonstrate my desire to do so?"

"My father and I lived together in a family. He loves me but he has never known what to do with me. If you think marriage and living in a home can solve these things like a magic trick, then you're wrong."

"So if I am not perfect I cannot try?" he asked, his voice fierce. And she went cold at that. Regretful.

"I didn't say that."

"You are asking me to tell you all that I can ever be before we have ever even heard the child's heartbeat. How does that strike you as fair?"

It wasn't. She knew that. She sighed.

"Love," she said. "What does it mean to you?"

They weren't in love. She knew that. She knew there was a difference between sex and feelings. She wasn't that naive. Yes, what had happened between them was amazing. But it hadn't been worth it. Not really.

She felt guilty for thinking that. She wanted to put her hand protectively over her stomach. Wanted to apologize to the little life blooming inside of her.

It hadn't asked to be created. She had to be sure that even though this wasn't planned she never passed on any resentment. It wasn't really a child that she resented. It was knowing that she had to solve this. That she had to take control of this and make it right. And standing in front of him right now with his demand of marriage hanging in the air she just wasn't sure what was right. More than that, she wasn't sure what her feelings were. But it felt disastrous.

She felt disastrous.

Wasn't this just the same? The same as it always was. He hadn't wanted her for her.

He wanted their child.

It was a hideous thing to be jealous of her own unborn baby, but there it was. It was never about her. He was even considering her father's feelings over hers.

It was just never about her.

"Does *marriage* mean something to you, then," she pressed. "If you can't tell me about love."

"It will mean, quite simply that you are my family. And if you are my family, then you will always be mine. I will take care of you. Always."

Taking care. It was what he saw from her father. That was how he interpreted the way her father provided for her.

That was hardly a declaration of love. But then, did she want one? She had imagined that she would get married someday, it just hadn't been anywhere near her radar. She had imagined that she might try and settle down in her thirties. And of course she had thought that it would be a union about love. Because otherwise what was the point?

Otherwise, why? Of course, there was a bigger answer to that question now. It was about the baby.

She wondered what her mother would do. Put in this situation. Her parents had loved each other very much. What would her mother have done if she had been faced with the prospect of marrying a man who didn't want to love, but wanted to create a family unit for the sake of their child. The truth was, life was fragile. And she had seen that firsthand. She had seen it at a young age. It had taken away some of the mystery and magic of life. The sense that things were charmed for her.

She had always thought that tragedy was something that befell others. And then it had befallen them. Their family, their kingdom had been shattered. And she'd had a little piece of life that was idyllic.

Sure, she was a nepo baby. But money didn't insulate you from tragedy.

If she married Dario, would she find that kingdom again? Or would it be impossible because it wasn't about love?

It is. It's about the love that you feel for your child. And how much you want that child to admire you.

Okay. That was true. But she just wanted to matter. If she had that business deal, then she would be an accomplished entrepreneur. She would be able to show her child what being a strong woman looked like. Maybe she wouldn't pale in comparison to Dario quite so much.

And that was the real issue. The rub. She didn't want to pale in comparison to Dario. She'd taken a step to finding a space to be different but effective with business, when it came to her father, but…she wanted to prove herself. She wanted to be special. Did she want everything? She kind of did.

"In terms of fidelity? Sex?"

"We have chemistry," he said. "I see no reason why we would have a marriage in name only."

The thought lit her on fire. She had been so convinced that those wild days in the snow were the only times they would ever have together.

But now he was talking about marriage. And sex. Sharing a life. Sharing a bed.

"And if you decide that you're tired of me?" she asked.

"I've never been with a woman long enough to tire of her."

"And so to that point you actually don't know how long it takes for you to get tired of a woman. If you do..."

"I'll let you know," he said.

If she ever became boring. If she ever had to be second to some random woman. The very idea made her feel sick.

"I won't be blindsided," she said. "Above all else, I won't be blindsided. I know what that's like. I was having a completely normal night. It was normal, and then my father came in to tell me that there was an accident and my mother was dead. And I have never gotten over that feeling. That you can be sitting there and everything will be just fine and the next moment your entire life is turned upside down. I will never sit there waiting for the other shoe to drop. Throw it to me first."

He nodded gravely and she was grateful she knew Dario was honest. Above all things, he was honest.

"You have my word. And the same applies to you. We can renegotiate the terms of the marriage at any time. But when it starts, we will be faithful. We will have a small child anyway."

She frowned. "Do you intend to be a hands-on father?"

"Yes. I do. Your father has been an incredible mentor to me. He is perhaps the only thing even near a father that I've ever experienced. I wish to give the same to our child."

"Yes, but you know small children don't want to hear about acquisitions and spreadsheets."

"I know that," he said.

"What if I tell you no?"

"You don't want to tell me no," he said. "Come now. Be reasonable. How would it benefit you to stay separate from me? Especially when I'm offering you a certain measure of freedom. You would rather walk into your father's office and tell him that you have decided not to marry me?"

"No," she said, suddenly and hideously appalled by that image. "I don't want to do that."

"I didn't think you did. And so here we are. At an impasse. Would you refuse for the sake of it? For the sake of your pride?" That galled her, because he was right. Half her issue was her pride. Half her issue was the fact that she didn't simply want to give him what he was asking for. It was a habit. Dario had vexed her for so many years it was difficult now to realize that she had to join forces with him. Even after those days they'd spent snowed in.

He had felt different then.

He had been such a wonderful lover. Courteous and generous and…

She needed to not think about that right now.

Was she going to do this? Agree to marry him and engage in all the spectacle that it would create? Agree to marry him and find herself back in his bed?

You want that.

She did. But she didn't want to want it. It was pointless. And worse, it was dangerous. What would happen if she ended up having feelings for him that he didn't return?

Isn't that already the case?

She shoved that thought to the side. She wasn't in love with him. But she did think about him quite a bit.

"Marry me," he said. "Join me. We will combine our companies and sit on top in business..."

Business. On top. Good God.

"You sound like Darth Vader, do you know that?" she asked, sounding a bit acidic.

He smiled. Looking grimly at her. "It is perhaps not a coincidence."

"Yes. Of course. You're so dark and bad."

Of course, saying that, even teasing made a little zip of arousal shiver through her. That was embarrassing. Really.

"Marry me," he said. "We will tell your father together. That he is going to be a grandfather, and that we are getting married."

"I..."

And she couldn't think of a reason not to. She absolutely couldn't.

Worst of all perhaps she wanted to say yes just for herself. But what would it get her? Well, this hot man would be her husband and they would spar ever after. But they would have a home and a child and perhaps that was all worth it?

Or maybe she was weak.

But if so, then she was weak.

She sighed.

"Well. How do you want to do this, then?"

"I'm canceling all of my plans, and we're going to dinner. I will then propose to you."

"Aren't you going to ask my father's permission?"

He frowned. "Neither of you would respect me if I did such a thing."

"It's traditional," she said.

"And you are not traditional. He may bluster about it, but he would rather I consult you than him. You know that, surely."

"I don't. But I'm glad that you do. Since he is clearly such a good friend to you."

"Don't be snappish," he said. "Go home and change. I will procure a ring for you, and then we will meet for dinner."

And that was how Lyssia found herself unofficially engaged, and stunned into complete silence.

CHAPTER NINE

DARIO'S MIND WAS working overtime to try and solve the intricacies of the situation. Of course, Nathan Anderson wouldn't be thrilled that Dario had gotten Lyssia pregnant out of wedlock, but he was a practical man, and he wouldn't be shocked by it. It wasn't as if he expected either of them to be chaste.

Pregnant.

She was pregnant with his child.

It had been all he could do not to threaten her. Threaten to take custody of the child, threaten to kidnap her. Beat his chest and climb the Empire State building like King Kong.

The problem was, this had hooked into something he hadn't known was in him.

He needed to make sure that there was every legal protection available to his child. He needed to make sure that no one could write scathing things about his child.

He needed to protect that child in all the ways that he wasn't protected, and marriage seemed the first step to doing that. Making sure that the circumstances surrounding his child's birth seemed clear. And he also didn't want to compromise his relationship with Lyssia's father. That was true too.

What does love mean to you?

There was no such thing as love. There was either care or no care. And he cared. He cared about that child. About its future. And he knew what it was like when a parent forfeited that care. It was unconscionable.

It was cold and lonely and memories he refused to have.

How long were you on the street?

Maybe a year.

He knew every night but he refused to name them.

He called a private jeweler immediately and had them bring a tray of engagement rings into his office.

Likely, he should have asked Lyssia what she wanted. But this was not about her.

It wasn't.

His body had reacted strongly when Lyssia had first come into the room, but after that, everything had been red.

Because the only thing that really mattered was doing the right thing for their child.

And yes, he would have her. Why wouldn't he? He was certainly not going to leave her celibate so that she could go off and make planned love to Carter.

No.

The child was his. She was his.

It all made perfect sense to him.

He chose the largest and most ostentatious ring. He

thought she would probably like it. There was nothing subtle about Lyssia. He thought about that white lingerie she'd worn the first time they were together. And the other outfits she'd worn in the times after.

He'd taken her in hot pink next to the shower. He'd stripped her of flimsy emerald green by the bathtub.

He bent her over the counter in the kitchen when she was in black, with matching heels.

He couldn't understand how she was pregnant. She'd said she was on the pill. He also knew that it was his child. Lyssia would never claim to be pregnant with his baby if it was someone else's. No. In fact, being pregnant with anyone else's baby would probably be an ideal situation for her. Then he called and arranged for a highly visible table at his favorite restaurant.

They would perform this. And when it was done, they would go and visit her father and tell him the news. As he sat at his desk, looking at the diamond ring, he called Lyssia. "I'll be at your house by six. We'll be having Italian."

"Well, that means it's probably going to be amazing," she said. "I doubt you would pick a bad Italian restaurant."

"You're correct. I am given to believe it is like old home cooking. I would hardly remember that. I barely remember what it's like to have a home in Italy much less anything cooked for me. But I like to think that my blood recalls."

"I assume I am to dress up?"

"Yes."

He got off the phone with her quickly, and cleared

his schedule for the next three days. There would be nothing but working toward assembling this wedding, and finalizing that business deal with her. He would not sign anything for it until they were married. Using it as a carrot was perhaps low, but it was necessary.

He wasn't sure which thing had gotten to her. The offer to join in business, or the comment about her father.

Because he did know that Lyssia cared very much what her father thought.

At a quarter to six he made his way to Lyssia's penthouse in Midtown, where he left his driver idling at the front and entered the code for the building. Of course he had it. Her father had given it to him in case there was ever an emergency.

This was the right thing to do. Not just for the child. Her father wanted him to take care of her. And this would not just protect their child, but her as well.

It was the right thing to do.

He went up the elevator to her floor, and walked down the hall. She opened it suddenly, her eyes wide. "What are you doing here this early?"

"I'm not early. Five minutes, maybe."

"Well, you didn't ask to be let up."

"I have a code. You didn't check to see who it was."

"I assumed it was somebody who works in the building. Or a neighbor."

She was half-dressed, wearing a silk nightgown.

"Are you all right?"

"Yes, I'm just… Trying to find something to wear."

"I can help."

"No thank you," she said.

"You don't think I have good taste?"

"I don't see the point of trying to look nice for a date with you if I then also show you all the things I try on. It doesn't actually make sense."

"It's not a date," he said. "We are putting on a performance."

"Right. Noted." He had clearly said the wrong thing. Or not. With Lyssia he could never really tell. Sometimes she acted put out just to fight with him.

"Don't be upset about it," he said. "You asked me what I think about love. I don't believe in it. Not as a philosophical concept. What I believe in is action. Taking care of the people that we have a responsibility to."

"Wow. Very romantic."

"I never said that it was romantic. But it is the truth."

"Why haven't you fallen in love with somebody yet? I mean, why didn't you have relationships in the past?"

She turned and walked toward her room. "You might as well come in," she said.

He walked in, and frowned. Her room was an explosion. Like her suitcase had been that first day. All of her things were strewn everywhere. And everything in the room was very pink.

"I never wanted a family," he said. "Or children. I have been single-minded and singularly focused since I was thirteen years old and decided to run away from the house I was being kept in." He was trying to decide if he should tell her the rest. Why not?

"There were children in that house. A married couple. The father was horrendously abusive. He beat me.

He beat his own children. He beat his wife. It was another place that I saw men abusing the position they were in. A position that should be sacred. What is less honorable than taking people into your care and causing them harm."

He had never told anyone this. There had never seemed a point. He wasn't sure if he wanted her to understand him or if he wanted to prove to her that everything she was so concerned about was silly.

He would be a good father.

A damned sight better than his own. It would be impossible not to be. But all of this going on and on about love.

"There's nothing honorable about that," she said softly.

"No. I was only ever given bad examples of what it means to be the head of the family. Of what it means to take care of a wife and child. I never wanted it. And I felt that my drive made me unsuitable to it. But now you are pregnant. And it is no longer a discussion. It is reality."

"Everything can be a discussion now, Dario. We live in a very flexible era."

She looked so sincere. He almost felt sorry for her. "Yes, *cara*, but I am not a flexible man."

She wrinkled her nose. "I mean, I know that. I've met you."

"Yes. I understand that. You know me. I feel that it has made you rather bold in your dealings with me. You do not understand, do you, Lyssia? The manner of man that I am. But you will. When you are mine, you will."

She would be his. His wife. He would have his wife and his child in his home, that he was certain of, and he would not yield.

He was not a man capable of such a thing.

"Yes. I know. You are a big, scary billionaire."

She reached down and grabbed a dress off the floor, and he lifted a brow as she shook it out. "Maybe this."

"How about not."

He stood and went over to her closet. A vast, walk-in room that was larger than some places he had stayed in his youth. His eye was caught by a long, red dress at the back. "That one."

"Which one?" She appeared in the doorway.

"Red. Tonight, you will wear red for me."

"I like pink," she said, because she always had to challenge him.

"I like red," he said, taking hold of her chin and holding her gaze steady on his. "You will do what I say. You will give me what I want."

He could see that she wanted to argue, but he could also see arousal flare in her eyes. The very things that irritated her about him were also the things that drew her to him. He could relate.

It was Lyssia's very nature that made her undeniable. Her buoyancy. Her quick wit and temper. It was also what made her an irredeemable brat. Sadly for him, he quite liked a brat.

At least, this particular brat.

"Leave," she said, shooing him out of the closet. A few moments later, she came out, the silken fabric of the dress molding to her body as a second skin. She wasn't wearing a bra and he could see the natural outline of her breasts, her nipples.

It was decent enough, but his eye was drawn there, and he couldn't look away.

He also didn't wish for her to change the way the dress was styled. Because it was far too intoxicating.

"Yes," he said. "That one."

"I'll just be a moment."

She emerged from the bathroom perhaps two minutes later, her blond hair put up in a carefree clip, a swipe of shimmer on her eyes, a bit of red on her lips. She was just so beautiful naturally that it took almost nothing to transform her into a glamorous goddess.

Truthfully, he could not have planned this better. He had not intended to take a wife, but what better wife then Lyssia Anderson? She was from this world. He had business dealings with her father, her father was the dearest mentor he had ever known.

She would be the hostess that he needed her to be when it came to having events. She would be the perfect accessory at any business affair.

Yes, this was actually much better than he had originally thought. He had been uncertain about it. But it would be…

It would be a boon. He would make sure of it. If there was one thing Dario was good at, it was making a boon out of a difficult situation.

And as for Lyssia… He was handling her as he always did.

"Let's go, *cara*. Our table awaits."

The car was waiting out front when they got downstairs, and he opened the door for her, pressing his hand to the small of her back as he guided her into the vehicle.

There was a barrier between them and the driver, so they were able to speak privately.

"This is going to create a little firestorm, isn't it?" she asked.

"Yes," he agreed. "It is. I have chosen a table in a location designed to help fuel that fire. You understand."

"It's very important to you that this looks a certain way."

"I will not have anybody speculating on my child being a bastard."

"I think we're a bit past that as a society, don't you?"

"Perhaps. But I am not from this world. And there will be people who say that your father should never have taken me in as he did considering I impregnated his daughter and did not make it right. They will say that I took advantage of you. They will talk about our age gap. The fact that I've known you for so long. The narrative will ever be that I am a predator from the streets who never should have been trusted."

"That isn't fair," she said, a small crease appearing between her eyebrows. "I was involved in making this baby just as much is you were."

"To be certain. And there will be plenty of things said about you. Sexism is alive and well. But so is classism. I am ever to be a hardscrabble success story. But with that success story comes the inevitable truth of my roots. And what people will say about them."

"Do you actually care?"

The question sent a fire through his blood. "Yes. I did not spend all these years remaking myself into something new only to be cast in the mold that I came out of. I destroyed that. Broke it. Very deliberately. I have made myself new. I made myself safe, and I will make my child equally so."

He had not meant to say quite so much, and he could see that she was rocked by what he had said.

"I didn't think of it that way."

"All I have ever wanted is to put as much distance between that danger and myself as I could. I will not pass it on to my heir. I will not send it down my bloodline."

She nodded slowly. "I understand that. I do. I'm sorry if it seems like I'm insensitive. It's…it's exhausting all of this, isn't it? We bat awful things back and forth with our verbal rackets and try to respond and get in our own truths and…there isn't time, it doesn't feel like. For me to take all this in because I'm listening to you but I'm also just trying to breathe. To survive this. It's all unknown. Being a mother. I want to have this baby but I'm terrified."

"Do you think you have the monopoly on fear?"

She shook her head. "No. Though you handle it differently than I do. But I understand why you're afraid."

"You have experienced challenges in your life. I'm not denying that. But you don't know what it's like. To continually feel that you have to earn a place."

She looked out the window, and then back at him. "Not in the same way you do. But I do feel like I always have to earn a place. My mother loved having a child.

It was, I think, the only thing she really wanted. My father would see me at dinnertime, and he enjoyed me, but it wasn't the same. I loved him. I love him. Please don't misunderstand. When my mother died, my father was bereft, and I could never shake the feeling that he had loved being her husband far more than he ever loved being my father. He never said that. But I always felt like I had to earn the right to still be there. To consume so much of his attention when what he wanted to do was sink into the sadness of having lost his wife, and I cannot blame him. I can't. He loved her so much. And I wanted to be able to fill that void, I wanted to be there for him. And then there was you. He met you, Dario, and it was like watching the light return to him. I think he always wanted a son. But he could never face the idea of marrying again. Because he would never love anyone other than my mother. And you were everything he ever wanted. And not a child. I think he never did know what to do with children. But an adult protégé who was good, better than he was, everything he valued? You were what healed him, not me. All I have ever wanted is to be the one bringing the light in, and I could never quite manage it."

She took a shuddering breath. "I'm not saying that I haven't had a certain amount of ease in my life. I have. And I'm not fool enough to think that I understand the struggle that you went through. I never had to do hard labor. I was never hungry. I was never afraid. I didn't move to a new country when I was a teenager and start over. I know that you did. But sometimes I felt invisible in my own house. I have always felt caught between all the things that I wanted. The love of my father, the desire for the right kind of success that would make him impressed with me, and the urge to be myself. Somewhere in all of that I think I never even quite figured out who I was."

It would be easy to brush these things aside. It would be easy to dismiss her as a poor little rich girl. But her pain was very real, and he did not relish it. It was the kind of pain he thought he might've had if his life had continued on in the normal fashion. If it hadn't been shattered so spectacularly. The kind of pain he might've experienced if his father had been human, rather than a monster who had abandoned his son. He and Lyssia were living in the fallout of things they could not control. They had both lost their mothers. They had both been left with fathers who had not been up to the task.

But her father had weathered it. He had stayed. His own had not.

Her pain was real. It didn't have to be about safety and survival to be real.

"You are every inch yourself," he said. "Whether you feel that or not. And I'm not certain that at twenty-three you're meant to fully understand who you are. Life has a way of changing our expectations, does it not?"

He was a decade older than she was, and yet he too was on the cusp of a profound change. She was going to be a mother and he was going to be a father.

A father.

There was no relationship on earth he had a more complicated feeling about.

Lyssia's father had been so good to him. His own so damaging.

He had vowed he would never be a father. Or a husband. Now he was to be both.

"I have gotten this far with great certainty of how everything would go. I never counted on you. On this. In that sense, perhaps neither of us know ourselves. Or at the very least we do not have great enough respect for how the world might intervene."

"Is it fate, do you think?"

"I think it was lust," he said. "Which has been undoing the greater plans of humanity for thousands of years."

She laughed softly. "Well. That's a good point. Though, not quite as romantic as fate." There was something hopeful in her eyes, and it made him ache. Because if she was hoping for real romance, there was no chance of him giving it. He thought of his own home. Back in Italy. Small and simple and filled with warmth.

His father had never been a bad man.

His father had always loved him. That was the frightening thing.

It was the truly frightening thing.

"Life is not overly romantic," he said. "And anyway, romance can be dangerous. I prefer to rest on careful planning."

"Isn't the topic of discussion about how plans fall apart?"

He smiled. "Then you make new plans."

"What is the saying, Dario? Man plans, God laughs?"

"Good thing I'm relatively adjacent to the divine, isn't it?"

"You have always been so arrogant. And I have always wanted to be more horrified by it than I am."

"What a tragedy for you, then, that you find me irresistible."

She looked at him and spread her hands. "Here I am, resisting."

"And after dinner?"

"Are we talking to my father after dinner?"

"Indeed."

"I'm going to guess that I won't be in the mood after that."

"We'll see." Because there was something about the bright burning between them that made him feel like this was something a little more familiar. Like it was something a bit more manageable.

The car pulled up to the restaurant then, the large picture windows lit up brilliantly, making the diners inside look as if they were part of a theatrical production.

Exactly perfect. Their table was right in the center.

"Let's go, then," he said, opening the door and getting out, and helping her out of the car. He put his arm around her waist, and she let out a small sound. He looked at her. "Yes?"

"I don't know. This is strange. We… We might've been together quite a bit when we were snowed in, but that wasn't real life. This… This feels more real. And it's scary. Different. Because you're Dario. And I…"

Her eyes glittered, and he had to look away. "It was

always going to be this way between us. I understand why you didn't see that." It wasn't like he had seen it either. He had great faith in his ability to resist her. Why wouldn't he? He had never been given any reason to suspect he wouldn't be able to resist their attraction. Because attraction when it came to feeling something for a specific woman had never meant much of anything to him. And yet, there she was. At his side, because he simply hadn't been able to turn away from the fire that built to his stomach every time he saw her.

He was undone by this woman that he had known all these years. And yet, had they truly known each other? There had been honesty between them. But it had been rooted in the present. In the moment. They'd volley back and forth and in those moments he felt he saw her, the her she really was. But this was different. They were peeling back layers, excavating each other's pasts, their feelings. Not a single person on earth knew these things about him. None but her.

He was as blindsided by all of it as she was, but he refused to let her know that.

Instead, he swept her into the restaurant where they were greeted by a spate of staff. "Bring us your specials," he said, as they took their seats.

"We're not even going to order off the menu?" she asked.

"No. You will trust me."

He wanted her trust, he realized.

Perhaps she wasn't the only one who still felt like she was earning her place.

He knew that she wasn't. If he wasn't still earning

his way, then he wouldn't feel so strongly about marriage. He wouldn't feel so strongly about making sure they did this in such a way that he was above reproach.

He didn't want their child reading stories about him being some sort of predator, of course. But he also just didn't want… He had worked hard to get where he was. And he didn't want baseless assumptions made about him. Not for any reason.

He had earned more than that.

It was impossible, he realized that, to completely avoid judgment in the court of public opinion. It was how the internet worked. Everyone had a method by which to share their opinions, and every opinion was treated as discourse, often printed in the news.

He would mitigate as much as possible.

Dinner was served, and Lyssia went straight for the bread, and the pasta, and he could tell by the look on her face that she agreed with his choices.

He watched her enjoyment and felt a strange sort of satisfaction regarding it. He had done this. He had satisfied her in this way. Yes, he had satisfied her sexually the whole time they were together at the chalet. But tonight, he had satisfied her in a different way. He was caring for her. Whether she knew it or not. And yes, some of this was to guard himself and his own reputation. But a substantial amount of it was about her.

He had, on a whim, earlier today, looked her name up online. He didn't care much for those things, though of course he had an awareness of his own reputation. It was part of managing his image. Which was part of good business.

He'd never looked her up. The internet was harsh and cruel about her. They saw her as a socialite playing at having a business, and he could see where much of her insecurity had come from. If her father didn't rush in to fill the void left by her mother, then those voices were going to do it.

He didn't want that for her. Perhaps, what he needed to do was begin to fill that void. With words of his own. Today, she had been a different version of herself than he had seen before. Confident and fiery. She had a plan. She'd been self-assured. The ability for her to do that had always been there. But she was afraid. Afraid to try because it might lead to rejection.

It was difficult to see that, because she spoke freely. At least, she did with him.

"I have seen now," he said. "Those online articles you were referencing before."

"Oh, the ones talking about how I'm bad at things?"

"Yes. They don't know you. They are strangers."

"Are you really going to talk to me about how public opinion doesn't matter when we're sitting here engaged in a big PR gambit?"

"I'm not going to talk to you about that. Public opinion does matter, to the extent that it affects your business. And for a child, I worry it would affect how they felt about themselves, about us. But it doesn't affect how I feel about myself. And I feel that you have been made to feel bad about yourself because nobody was working to say good things to you. Positive things. You proved today that you were capable of putting together an amazing business plan. You are smart. Talented.

Capable. You're artistic. You design the furniture and the home goods yourself, do you not?"

She was the mother of his child. And further to that she'd asked what he would do to support their child. So that their child didn't feel like she did. So that he didn't repeat the mistakes her father had made, and God knew, he didn't truly think he was a better man than Nathan Anderson. But he wanted to try.

"Yes," she said. "Everything in my apartment is something from my collection. You should… You should come see my studio sometime."

"You're right. I should."

He was not creative. He was good at building things. And not hiring the right people to design them. To execute them. People were his talent.

Lyssia seemed to have many talents, and she was not given credit for that.

"What made you decide to design these things?" He would never have thought of it. It was interesting. He felt big, he was good at that. But the truth was, it had been a natural extension for him to go into the business he had because he had come up working in hospitality.

"I…" She looked down, her cheeks turning the same color crimson of her lips.

"Tell me," he said. "Whatever it is inspired you to start a company. Whatever it is you have taken that inspiration and created many beautiful things with it. I want to know."

She smiled, lovely. Warm. It made something bloom within him.

"My mom loved to decorate. I associated all of these little touches around the house with her. They stayed the same for long time afterward. And then after I left the house, my dad sort of redid everything and made it very Spartan. He didn't add decorations. He didn't put knickknacks on shelves. He didn't have decorative lamps. I associated touches of home, of warmth with her. It can make you feel certain things. It can change your whole mood. I thought if I could help people change their surroundings, I can help them change the way that they felt. There is something about an attention to detail that can really create a whole new environment. I know my bedroom was really messy. But my house is stylized, but lived in. I don't like things to be to Spartan. It reminds me of... Of loss."

"I can think of few other better reasons to do anything."

He sat there watching, holding the stem on his wineglass between his thumb and forefinger, turning it absently. "I think one reason I was drawn to hospitality, other than the fact that a cruise ship allowed me to gain entry into the United States, was that it was about comfort. I had a shortage of it. For many years. And there was something about being able to give it to somebody else, and by doing that work, earning money so that I can have some myself, that gave me a sense of purpose. And of pride. I do not create things like you do. But it was still a lack of something that drew me to this life. I can do anything now. I could stop working.

I could buy a different company. Get into a new sort of industry. I like what I do now."

"Do you… I know that you care a lot about the environment."

He sniffed. "It's expedient to be seen as doing so."

"Yes, your street cred is safe with me. I think you care about it. What other charities do you give to?"

"It isn't important," he said.

"Ah, so there are charities." She looked far too pleased with herself for divining that information. He found her irritating.

"I don't see what business it is of yours."

"We're sharing information. Having a conversation. Like humans. Humans that are about to be engaged."

"I have a foundation. I don't advertise it. For homeless youth. And another for general housing and security. We've had old hotels and apartment buildings renovated into affordable housing. And we give classes, to help people reenter society. One of the things people don't realize about growing up in that way, or living that way for a certain number of years, is that it isn't quite so simple as just deciding to step back into society. You have to learn. I was good at that. I was good at watching people and figuring it out on my own. But not everybody is. I was able to come up with a very convincing facade. One that helps me convince people that I belonged wherever I was. I don't take that for granted. Nor do I expect for everyone to be able to do it."

"You're a very compassionate person," she said.

He wanted to push against that. He had never thought of himself as compassionate. He had only ever thought of himself as practical. It wasn't right that people suffer on the streets if they wanted a different life. It wasn't right that children should suffer because of the choices that their parents had made. He didn't believe that people should be thrown away like garbage, he didn't consider that compassion, he considered it reasonable.

"Don't spin fantasies about me. I am the man that you have always known. The man you disliked this entire time. And now that I have given you pleasure, you seem to like me more."

"That isn't all you did. I'm having your baby."

"Yes, well. Don't go trying to spin that into a better situation by creating stories about me. I am still the man that you've known all this time. The one that you found cold and cruel at times."

"But you're also the man that I got to know in the chalet. You are also a man who hasn't forgotten where he came from. Maybe I shouldn't romanticize you, but isn't it fair to say that you're more than you've shown me?"

"You make it sound as if I have done something deliberate with you, and I have not." He chose his words carefully. Because they were sharp enough that they would slice beneath her skin, and she might not feel it just now. But she would later.

"None of this has been a game. And none of it has been a plan. I was not hiding something and then showing you. I did not think of you at all. I thought of myself. My own comfort, and my own enjoyment."

"Liar," she said.

Later. It would hurt later. It would make her think later.

The dessert came, and as soon as she finished the last bite, he moved from his chair and got down on one knee. "Lyssia, *cara*, will you marry me?"

CHAPTER TEN

UNTIL HE'D GOTTEN down on one knee, she'd forgotten it was a farce. Well, it wasn't a farce. She was really going to marry him because she was really having a baby.

But for a moment, they had just felt like two people who were connecting. Talking. Like two people who had chosen to share each other's company, rather than what they were. Two people performing a very specific farce for the world. One that had nothing to do with how he listened to her or made her feel validated or interesting. One that had nothing to do with her at all. It was all about him. Him and his reputation. And as he lifted the lid on the velvet box that contained the engagement ring, she forgot to breathe. Because she was struck dumb by how hurt she was. By how unfair this felt.

Because it was beautiful, this moment. Because she realized she felt some things for him that she would rather not. At this inopportune time.

Where he was there, being gorgeous and all the things he ever was, but fundamentally not… Hers.

She'd said yes to him. To this. But the enormity of the emotional mountain that separated them was so vast she didn't see how they could ever overcome it. And worse, he wouldn't want to.

And she had no choice. No choice but to smile. No choice but to extend her hand while everyone in the restaurant looked on. And he took the most enormous ring she had ever seen out of the box and slid it onto her finger. She had never imagined this moment. Not really. Right then she realized it could only have ever been with him.

Because something about Dario had gotten under her skin and stayed there from the moment she'd first seen him.

Yes, when they'd first met she'd been a child, and it hadn't been at all like that. But she had lost someone then. And then… He had been there.

He had felt like arrival in many ways, and sometimes he still did.

He was significant, though. In a way she wouldn't be able to easily describe to anyone.

Right then, it felt confusing. Right then it felt horribly, and terribly poignant.

If she were going to write an article about it, then it would be a fairy tale.

They had known each other all of their lives. They were so different. They had both lost their mothers.

They had always been sparring partners. But then they'd become lovers.

They had fought their way through personality clashes and misunderstandings through an attraction that was undeniable. He had listened when she needed someone to talk to. He had encouraged her to be the best version of herself.

She only needed him to be him.

She made him tell her the nicer things about himself. Made him admit that he was a human and not a robot.

But that wasn't the truth.

It was just all the beautiful clues that he had strung together to lead to this moment. The assumptions that would be employed in order to make all of this seem magic. Rather than cold and calculated.

And part of her still felt caught up in it. Part of her still wanted to weep. Part of her still wanted to pretend that it was a fairy tale.

He stood, then lifted her up out of the chair and pulled her into his arms.

He hadn't touched her like this in six weeks.

The restaurant was their captive audience, and she had no time to respond before he brought his mouth down to hers, kissing her deep and long. Kissing her with intensity.

She clung to his arms, to keep herself from falling, from melting into a puddle at his feet. God knew she possibly might.

His mouth was firm and knowing. Not just of sex in general, but of her. As if he could reach in and read the deepest, most personal fantasies that she had.

His tongue swept hers, and she was transported. Back to that moment in the chalet when it had just been them.

This pure sort of reckoning of all that existed between them.

And when it was over, she felt dizzy, and displaced. Resentful that they were here in New York, and not back in their own cocoon.

But this was now. It was reality. They were having a baby. They were getting married. Her life was completely different now from how it had been. Her future was going to be something entirely separate to what she had imagined it would be.

Everything. Everything was different.

She had no idea how to reconcile that.

She wasn't even sure she wanted to. There was something almost comforting in the feeling of being outside of her body. Almost comforting in not feeling like herself. Not feeling like it was real.

"We should get to your father's as soon as possible. We don't want him to see it on the news."

"It'll probably just be on social media," she said. "And he won't see that."

He chuckled. "True."

She didn't know how he could laugh. She didn't know how he could be relaxed in any way. She felt like she was at the end of herself.

And she found herself being whisked out of the restaurant and back to his town car.

Being chauffeured out of the city and headed toward her father's house upstate.

It was an hour's drive, and she didn't quite know what to say as they burned through the miles on the highway.

"We will marry as soon as possible."

"We need to be able to actually put a wedding together," she said.

"The wedding doesn't matter," he said.

"How can you say that? After going to such great lengths to organize that spectacle of an engagement, how can you think that the wedding won't matter?"

"A small intimate ceremony with family and friends," he said as though he was reading the headline.

"Maybe that isn't what I want. Maybe I want to have an actual wedding. Did you ever think about that?"

"No," he said. "Have you?"

"No. I actually haven't thought that much about my wedding."

She leaned back against the seat.

Her father would give her away. Her mother was dead.

It actually made her want to cry.

"I want a dress, and I need it to be exactly right, and I want decorations and..."

"If you want a gorgeous dress then you are going to have to marry me sooner rather than later, because fit is going to become an issue."

She made an exasperated sound.

"I liked you better when you were pretending to be my date," she said.

She could see the intensity in his dark eyes as he looked at her in the dim light of the vehicle. "I wasn't pretending. I am actually interested in you. I do want to see your studio."

"Speaking of my studio, and my apartment, I assume that you expect me to move in with you."

"Yes. Though my penthouse in Manhattan is not far from yours, if you wish to maintain a studio in your space, and have an option for a place to sleep, that is fine with me."

He was being so reasonable. That was maybe the most annoying thing. That she wanted to rage at him, because he was making her feel raw and he was making her feel sensitive, but he was being perfectly… Correct. About so many things. The fact that he had held the business deal over her head was almost a courtesy. Because the truth was, she never would've been able to face her father telling him that she was pregnant with Dario's baby, and wasn't marrying him.

She hadn't really been able to think about that. She'd had to scale Mount Dario first.

But Dario knew.

Dario knew that she would never have been able to stand that. He knew that it would make her feel far too much like a disappointment. Like she was letting everyone down. Him and her father. He knew that, and he had known it was actually the only ammunition that he needed. So yes. Yet again, he was being far more reasonable than she would like. She would like some goads to kick against. It made her feel alive. She liked it when Dario was that way, because she felt like a piece of iron sharpening another piece of iron. Or at the very least, she didn't feel vulnerable. And right now, she felt a bit vulnerable. And he got to be charitable. Giving her the kind of arrangement that would make her feel safe and protected. Giving her something for her business so that she could look more accomplished than she was.

A sliver of uncertainty worked its way beneath her skin.

The thing was, he had said it, and she hadn't fully understood it. He hadn't really tailored himself to her either way. He wasn't really thinking of her. She had taken that to mean that he wasn't being manipulative, at least in the moment. Now it felt like maybe she was incidental, and it left her wounded. Breathless.

Finally, they pulled up to her father's palatial estate. The lights were on, and she knew that he was still awake. He had always been the sort of man who ran on very little sleep. He liked to work. And he liked to research things.

No wonder he and Dario got along so well. There was an intensity to both of them that just seemed a natural part of who they were. Her own father had never been hungry. Not in the way that Dario was, and yet it had been a natural thing for him to build and build and build his empire.

As natural as breathing.

And Dario… He had that spark that her father had, and yet he had been keen. Not just to survive, but to thrive. He had made a difference, not only in his own life, but in the lives of so many other people.

It really was no wonder that her father esteemed Dario so highly. Above anyone else on earth. She was just such a disaster. She'd been so confident there for a bit. And now life was…unrecognizable.

"Did you warn him that we were coming?"

"I did. I told him that we would see him tonight."

"Did you give him any indicator..."

"That I got you pregnant? No."

"How is it we are going to do this? Are we going to do both in the same breath? I'll be going to lead with the marriage..."

"The engagement, obviously. The news about the grandchild will come after that."

"For someone who doesn't have a lot of family, you have some decent insight into how to manage them."

That, she realized, landed a little bit more roughly than she had intended to.

"I didn't mean..."

"It's fine," he said. "I am aware that I am a functional orphan. I'm at peace with it."

They got out of the car and went to the front door.

Her father unlocked it without waiting for them to knock.

And there he was, waiting in the entry. She felt the need to hide her hands behind her back, because the ring suddenly felt so conspicuous it seemed like he would know before they ever even announced it.

Not that it was a bad thing, it was just... She was so near nervous. It was entirely unfathomable to her that only two months ago she would've said Dario was the most annoying man on earth, and now she was marrying him.

She still felt like he was the most annoying man on earth, but the marriage part was a real shift.

Her father would no doubt be shocked. He would probably figure out that they were getting married because of the baby. Would he be disappointed in her? Disappointed that she had lost her head and let her hormones prevail?

They had been responsible. Well. They hadn't really been irresponsible. She was on birth control, and it should've worked. It was just that it hadn't. And… And.

She felt a little bit faint.

"To what do I owe the visit?" her father asked.

In his early sixties, Nathan Anderson was still handsome and filled with energy.

"We have something to tell you," said Dario, plying her left hand out from behind her back. "Lyssia and I are engaged."

Her father looked stunned. The whole ten seconds, he didn't move.

"Well," he said. And then he took a step forward and gripped her by the shoulders. "That is the most wonderful news." He pulled her in and hugged her, and suddenly, Lyssia felt the urge to see if it was possible to break the moment. She didn't want to settle into this. Into her father's joy if it was only going to be compromised.

"I'm pregnant." She announced this, as if she was announcing that she was taking a nice trip down to Saks Fifth Avenue.

"Pregnant," her father said. He pulled away from her and looked to Dario, and then back at Lyssia. Here it was. Now he would rail. Now he would be angry.

"I'm going to be a grandfather," he said. He moved to Dario then, and clapped him on the shoulders. "You have made me a grandfather," he said. "My son."

She looked at Dario's face, and saw a myriad of emotions there. Unreadable. Unknowable. She felt a similar kaleidoscope in herself, because her dad was more invested right then in Dario than her and it galled, but she also knew Dario needed it, and that mattered. "I cannot tell you how happy this makes me. I never could have dreamed of such wonderful news. Was it being snowed in together?"

"That certainly was a factor," said Lyssia, her face getting hot.

Dario lifted a brow and gave her a scolding look.

"But there was always something about him," she said.

Because it was true anyway.

Dario moved, putting his hand on her lower back. "I have always been very fond of Lyssia. And I wanted to be very careful, because she's younger than me. Because I esteem you so much. Both of you. I never would have wanted to play lightly with her feelings. But I have been quite taken with her for a while. It was only spending uninterrupted time together that allowed us to understand what our connection really is."

"I don't need to know the details," her dad said. But he was smiling. "When is the wedding?"

"The sooner the better. We've known each other many years. There's no reason to delay," said Dario.

"Well, but we will want to have it in the Hamptons."

"I was thinking Rome," said Dario.

Rome? The place where he'd been homeless? Why? But now wasn't the time to ask.

"Rome," her father said. "That is a good idea."

"I know just where. It will overlook the sea. Don't worry about a thing. I will handle it all. And there will be no reason that the preparations should take more than two weeks. Whatever dress you want can be made, Lyssia," he said, cutting off her protests.

She blinked, but didn't say anything.

"Lyssia," her father said. "I have truly never been prouder."

Lyssia felt like she had been stabbed. Right through the chest. Because somehow, it was something to do with Dario that made her father the proudest. It wasn't her job. It wasn't simply being her. It was incubating Dario's child.

It is your child too.

Yes. But it didn't feel like it. Everything felt… She just felt so raw.

She didn't know what to do about it. Didn't know how to combat these feelings inside of her.

"Let's have a drink."

They did. They ended up staying and having a drink with her father, and then after an hour, Dario said that they had to go. "It will take us an hour to get back to the city," said Dario. "We should head back."

"Of course, of course. Keep me posted on the wedding plans."

"We will."

"Lyssia," her father said. "Send me over the proposal for your redesign for the hotels."

That at least cheered her slightly. "I will."

"Of course I know you'll be very busy now. With your baby. You will be a wonderful mother."

It was perhaps the most definitively encouraging and kind thing he'd ever said.

They got back into the car, and she leaned her head back against the seat. "Don't worry," he said. "We're not going back to the city."

"Why did you tell my father we were?" she asked.

"Because he does not need to know that I intend to take you to a luxury bed-and-breakfast where I plan on sealing this arrangement in a very particular way."

The way that he looked at her. That dark need in his eyes.

It was the first thing that made her feel like she might have some control here. And yet at the same time it made her feel undone.

They wanted each other. At the end of the day, it was her real power, and his.

They could claim all sorts of things. That by her agreeing she was making things easier with her father, that by him giving her the business deal he was improving her situation.

But mostly, she had the feeling they wanted each other. And if she didn't have him, some other woman might. If he didn't have her, perhaps other men would have her.

Maybe this was the truth of it. And that was both deeply comforting and confronting all at the same time.

"I am sorry, Lyssia," he said, softly.

"For what?" she asked.

The only sound was her heart beating and the tires on the road.

"I...feel as if I got more attention in that moment. And I am not... I am not his son."

He finally saw it. She felt bad, though, because while she'd had her own conflicting feelings about it...she hated everything she knew about Dario's childhood. She didn't begrudge him a relationship with her dad.

"I was happy," she said. "Happy that he's happy."

"But he should have been all there for you."

"He cares for you. It doesn't have to be a competition."

"But it has felt like one to you and that matters to me," he said. "We...you and I, we are a family now. This baby will be ours. There is nothing more important. Know that."

She held that close and turned it over. This small change in him. This insight. It mattered. But she had to resist the urge to make it more than it was.

They only drove five minutes away from her father's house, and up to a glorious, rambling manor. "I rented the northern wing for us."

They walked inside, and she was struck by how quaint it was. How lovely. The walls were hunter green, with brown leather details all about the room. Hunting and fishing memorabilia from a bygone era added a warmth and a sense of another time to the place.

He went up to the polished mahogany desk and the woman behind the desk presented them with physical keys. They were given directions to the far side of the house. Where a library, a sitting room and a large bedroom with an en suite bathroom was theirs.

Two suitcases seemed to be produced from thin air, though she realized they had to come from the car.

"Did you… Take clothes from my house?"

"No," he said. "I purchased some things for you."

"Well, that…" She tried to muster up a fence, and instead she was intrigued. What sorts of things did Dario think that she should wear? Lyssia had a very strong sense of style. What did Dario see? That was the question. Of course, that was just a distraction from the actual, prevailing thought pounding through her. She was going to make love with Dario again.

And when he led her through the public area, back to the quarters that they would share. She didn't wait. Didn't hesitate. As soon as the door closed behind them, she stretched up on her toes, and she kissed him.

CHAPTER ELEVEN

DARIO HAD KNOWN that this was self-indulgent. But it was, in many ways, a fool's decision. But he could not go back. And wouldn't even if he could. Because the moment that he tasted Lyssia's mouth again, he wanted nothing else.

It had been torment tonight, standing with her in front of her father and keeping his hands to himself. Playing at being respectable. Not exposing the fact that the reason they were in the situation, the reason that they were getting married was because of the undeniable passion between them. Not feelings.

And then…and then her father had overlooked her, in his opinion, and everything in him had been twisted, turned sideways. It was all complicated and he didn't want that now. He wanted it simple.

He wanted her.

He wanted her to know she was his.

Maybe there was never going to be a way to untangle the emotional threads from all of this. But he wanted to stamp her, claim her, make her certain that she was his so that she would never look…hollow and alone as she had for a moment standing there in her father's entry.

He growled, moving his hand to her hair and pulling hard, drawing her head back, kissing her throat, down her collarbone.

She let out a sharp gasp.

"You are mine," he said. Something primitive was rioting through him. Something that made him feel like a stranger even to himself.

He wanted her. He was no stranger to sexual desire, but this was something else entirely. This was like a foreign entity had taken him over. This was something he was at the mercy of. And that was an entirely unfamiliar concept.

He couldn't wait. He was starving for her. He stripped her naked, bared her gorgeous body to his gaze.

The dress she had on was beautiful, but it had nothing on her bare skin.

Her breasts were full, pink tipped and lush.

He was held captive by the sight of the pale thatch of curls between her thighs.

His sex grew heavy with need, his heart pounding so hard he thought it would make its way out of his chest entirely.

She was everything.

"Take your hair down," he commanded.

He moved to a wingback chair in the corner and sat, watching her.

She was still wearing her high heels, her legs looking endless in those.

She reached behind her and undid the clip, let her blond hair fell down past her shoulders.

"Very good," he said. "I think that you should bring me a drink, Lyssia."

She looked at him, challenges parking in her blue eyes. "Why?"

"To see if you're any sweeter now that the promise of pleasure is before you. Sweeter than you were back when you were my assistant."

He felt compelled to marry those moments. This glorious need that he felt for her, combined with those past interactions. With that moment that he had first noticed her beauty when she'd walked into his office. When she had brought him the coffee and spilled it, gotten down on her knees before him.

"What would you like, Mr. Rivelli?" she asked, her voice sultry.

A satisfied, masculine sound sounded short and sharp in his throat. "Whiskey. Neat."

"Anything for you."

Still wearing heels, she walked to the sideboard and grabbed a bottle of amber liquid, pouring a measure of it into a tumbler. Then, with one hand at the bottom of the cup, and the other at the top, holding it as though she was grandly presenting, she made her way to him, her eyes never leaving his.

He took the whiskey from her hand.

"Do you remember, the day you came into my office, and spilled coffee all over the floor?"

"Yes," she said. "I was mortified."

"I wasn't. I was consumed by fantasies of you. You

got on your knees before me, and all I could think of was how glorious your lips would look if they were wrapped around me."

She looked at him, her eyes dewy, full of questions.

"Get on your knees, Lyssia. Kneel before me."

At first he thought she would argue. And that would be its own kind of pleasure.

But she didn't. Instead, she went down in front of him. He moved his hands to his belt, undid his slacks. It freed his arousal. She leaned in, her lips brushing against the sensitive head of him.

"Take me in your mouth," he said.

She didn't argue. Finally, Lyssia obeyed him. Beautifully. Sweetly. She wrapped her hand around the thick base of his shaft and took him into her mouth. Sucking him slowly.

Then she began to lick him like he was her favorite sweet.

Over and over again she took him like that. And he gripped her hair, steadying himself. Steadying them both.

He thrust his hips upward as she moved over him.

A swilling supplicant, naked before him.

She seemed bound and determined to take his pleasure that way.

"No," he said.

He lifted her, and brought her down onto his lap, bringing the heart of her to the blunt head of his arousal. He lowered her slowly onto him, until she was fully seated with him deep inside.

She let her head fall back, the sound of need emanating from her throat. She was wet. Unbearably so. Gloriously turned on by what had just happened between them.

She braced herself on his shoulders and she began to move. Rocking back and forth, and up and down over his length.

He had given the order, but she held him in thrall now.

"Lyssia," he growled.

And he lost himself. In the feel of her. The tight clasp of her body. That warm, wet heat.

All that glory.

Like he had never known.

They would marry for their child. For the public. For her father. But this, this was for them. When she had asked him what he would do if he tired of her he had lied. Because he would never tire of her. She was his. Utterly and completely. He had never had anything that belonged to him quite like this.

He had everything that he wanted that money could buy. That much was true.

But there was not a single person he could lay claim to.

He made connections, and he made them with ease. He had not connected with Lyssia using charm. He had not used his powers of assimilation. He had not given her only what she wanted to see. Their connection, from the beginning had been more real. The antagonism of it all more honest.

And that made this more.

He had charmed her into bed.

They had not played a game to get to this moment. What happened between them had been real. It had been undeniable.

It still was.

She brought herself down on him again and again. He didn't want it to end. He wanted to delay the moment of inevitable release for as long as possible. He wanted her. Only her. Always and ever her.

He moved his hand between their bodies, stroked the source of her pleasure there. Then captured it between his fingers and squeezed. She unraveled. Her pleasure a victory that he needed badly to win. Because finally, then and only then, did he surrender to his own need. Did he give himself over to the untamed thing inside of him.

Only then did he let himself go. Utterly and completely, his orgasm his undoing. In a way that nothing ever had been. She was singular. She was dangerous. He had never wanted in this way before. Even right after having her, he wanted.

He had dropped the whiskey. He had forgotten about it. It was on the floor, spilled, and there was something about that which felt symbolic in some regard. She had dropped the coffee the day he had first seen her.

And he was no longer aware of anything but her on this day. This day that she was bound to him. To marry him.

She would be his.

Unquestionably.

He looked at her, stroking her hair. "You're beautiful," he said. Because there was nothing deeper that he knew how to say.

"So are you," she said, her eyes looking sleepy.

"How do you find this?" he asked, stroking her cheek. "This association between the two of us. I am not Carter."

She blinked. "Who?" Then she laughed. "Seriously. I barely thought of him. It's probably unkind of me. But he and I never actually had a real commitment to each other. In fact, I think I might have overexaggerated the connection a little bit. I didn't want him. I wanted my life to feel different. I wanted to feel different. But in a way that I could control."

There was something about her words that resonated in him. He could understand them. He was a man who had remade himself so many times. Who had created a smoother, more polished veneer with each and every iteration. He understood that.

The knowledge that he could no longer be what he'd once been. The knowledge that he needed to be something more.

More than himself. More than the people around him.

It fascinated him that a woman like Lyssia, who'd had things he had only ever dreamed of, could feel that same way. He had, these many years, imagined that he was unscathed by his life. After all, he was a billionaire. He was successful. He was well known. Highly regarded, in general.

He was fine, in other words. Except he could see the little ways in which Lyssia was cracked by the losses in her own life. By the wounds even a loving father had left behind.

"Is this what you had in mind? Because things are different now."

"I'm not in control of this," she said.

She moved her hands to his shirt, and began to undo the white buttons. She pressed her palm beneath the fabric, smoothing it over his skin. "But neither of us are, are we?"

Her words held a dangerous and reckless edge, and he felt them. They went deep.

"I want you," he said. It was the closest he could give her to confirmation.

"I know," she said. "I want you. It's a hideous thing, isn't it? We used to have lives. And they weren't about this."

"I only thought of you most of the time," he said.

She laughed. "Only *most* of the time? You did better than I did. I wanted… I wanted to call you so many times while we were apart. But it just seemed like a bad idea. I thought you were done with me."

"I intended to be," he said. He shrugged. "When I was a child… I never knew what might happen next. As a man I have sought to make my world one I can control. It's been a long time since life has surprised me in any fashion. I suppose I should thank you. For this. It is at least something entirely different."

And he had control now. He knew himself. He knew better than to let himself believe wholly in the fiction of everything around him.

When he was a child he hadn't known better. He

had believed that his father loved him, and he had believed that love was a certain thing. Because his mother had told him that it was. His father had told him that it was. But when everything had gone wrong, his father hadn't protected him, he had sold him. Love had become something bitter. A betrayal. He would never believe in it again. Thus, in the decisions that he was making in regard to their child, he was using his head. Not his heart.

When it came to Lyssia, it was his body.

He could rationalize those things. And he found that to be very important.

Essential, even.

It was different from what he had imagined. But it wasn't beyond the boundaries that he had set forward for himself.

"Is that why you wish to marry in Rome?" she asked.

"Is what why?"

"More surprises?"

Something shifted within him. "Perhaps I just wish to return with everything in hand. Wealth, my wife, my child."

She shifted against him, but didn't speak.

"You should move in with me when we get back to Manhattan."

"I should?"

"Yes. It will be more convenient."

"For sex."

"Yes," he said. "What else would I mean?"

"Living with another person isn't only about sex. We

will be sharing things. Our lives." But the whole time she was talking she was moving her hand beneath his shirt. Lower and lower still.

"You want to live with me. You want to be with me," he said. "In my bed."

"You're very arrogant," she said.

"Yes," he said. "I am."

"You want me to live with you because you can't bear to be apart from me. Because you want me naked, all the time. How long has it been, Dario? Has it really been since I spilled the coffee in your office?"

"Yes," he said, his voice hard. "I wanted things from you that I knew then you could not even fathom. You were an adult, yes, but only technically. I was stunned by your beauty. And that is a rare thing. Because beauty is subjective. And it is everywhere. But there was something more with you. From the beginning. I wanted you."

"You should've had me then."

"A bad idea. I don't think you would've wanted to be my eighteen-year-old wife and mother to my child."

She laughed. "No. I am less of an idiot now than I was then."

"You will move in with me," he said.

"Yes. Of course. And I'll vacuum naked and in heels."

"Really?"

"Only if you cook me dinner naked."

"Sounds dangerous," he said. He gripped her chin. "Also, I have staff for that."

She laughed. "I do hope that your staff isn't naked."

"Of course not." But he did make a mental note to have there be clear times when no one else was in the house so that they did not always have to wear clothes.

He had never lived with a woman before.

Had never even thought about it.

It was a strange prospect. But one he quite liked. When the woman in question was Lyssia. She was interesting. She would perhaps be even more interesting in proximity.

"We didn't even make it to the bedroom."

"Feel free to lead the way. And explore what I brought in the suitcase."

Interest flared in her eyes.

There had been very few times in his life that Dario had ever considered himself happy. But right then, he felt like he might be.

CHAPTER TWELVE

THE NEXT MORNING, they spent some time wandering around the grounds of the bed-and-breakfast.

They had a leisurely meal in their quarters, and then began the drive back to Manhattan.

Lyssia felt like she was floating. And she had never especially felt like that before. She had never considered herself a romantic. Not really. But she was beginning to recognize that as being part of her very specific defense system.

It was not, she realized, in her nature to want everything.

Well. That wasn't true.

She did secretly want everything. It was just that she was afraid of putting too much of herself into it.

It was why Carter had seemed like a good idea.

He had seemed like a good idea because he had seemed safe. And ultimately, being safe was something that she valued perhaps more than having everything.

She'd realized that in some small part the first moment her lips had touched Dario's. But it was all becoming clearer as time went on.

She was happy. She didn't know what it meant. But she was hopeful, even, about the potential future.

About what they might have.

He was difficult to read sometimes. But so was she.

It wasn't like she was completely and totally emotionally available.

The truth was, she was somewhat stunted. It was because of her dedication to keeping things easy. Shallow.

She had tried having a business, and it wasn't like she hadn't put genuine heart into it. She had. Everything she had done had been genuine. Had been filled with actual effort. It was just that on some level, she had been holding back.

And she cared so much about what she did. The conversation she had with him at the restaurant had been clarifying in that regard. She wanted people to have a home the way that she did. She wanted everyone to be able to feel the kind of comfort that she'd once had. Including herself.

And when they arrived back at her apartment, she decided that she was going to show him everything.

"My studio… My office is in here."

She had a feeling that to the deeply organized Dario her method would seem haphazard. She looked around the room as someone who was unfamiliar with the place would. Taking in the bright pink walls, the patterned wallpaper that went up the wall her desk was flat against. Replete with palm fronds and birds of paradise. She knew that it was eclectic. To say the least. There were fabric swatches everywhere.

Wood stain samples, glaze swatches, and any and many other things.

"This is it," she said. "I do most of the basic designs in here."

He was speechless, looking around the space, and she could imagine that part of the issue was he couldn't picture himself getting any work done here. She knew him. His workspace was always neat as a pin. Hers was… A bit haphazard.

"It's quite amazing," he said. "What do you sketch your designs on?"

"Anything," she said, surprised that he hadn't made a comment about her organization. "Everything. I have notebooks. And I like to put different fabrics next to the sketches. Sometimes I do it all in a virtual notebook, and then I can take fabric that I have imported into the tablet and get a good idea for how it will look virtually."

"Do you design some of the textiles?"

"Yes," she said. "This is my range. No one else has these fabrics."

He moved over to the fabric swatches and touched them.

"I can make exclusive textiles for your hotel chain," she said.

"You don't have to."

"I want to," she said keenly. "I want this to be important. Special."

"This is quite impressive, Lyssia. You should consider hiring more people."

"I have a good team. They all work remotely. I have

people that liaise with manufacturers. I share some of the design work with a group of people."

"You haven't communicated much with them since I've been around you."

"Well, when I went to the chalet I was honestly thinking the whole business was winding down. I was ready to let it go. I felt like a failure."

"What changed your mind?"

"It really was talking to you. Well, and discovering I was pregnant. I was on the pill for my… For my periods, though, and it was a low dose. I have never tested it before, obviously. It turns out for me that wasn't sufficient. But you can bet I had a fight with my doctor about it. I spent three weeks going over and over what I was going to do. I was afraid to see you. I also missed you. I'm not used to going that long without seeing you. And we don't even usually talk or anything, but after the chalet I just…"

"I missed you," he said. "Even though you are a pain in the ass."

She felt flushed with pleasure over him saying that. It was perhaps the nicest thing Dario had ever said. "I really didn't expect that you would want to get married. Which is foolish, isn't it? You are very traditional down in your soul."

He seemed to withdraw from her then, even though he didn't move one bit. She could feel it. "I don't act out of a place of tradition. But security. What I am doing is for the good of our child. Here's what must be done. I will never let a child of mine suffer as I did, and that is not for the sake of tradition. And it could never be for feelings. Love is a foolish pursuit, Lyssia. It fails when we need it most. I believe in legally binding agreements. I do not believe in feelings. That is what has driven me here. Will continue to drive me. It is not tradition. It is practicality."

She felt wounded by that. And she was reminded again of what he had said to her. But he did not do any of this for her.

And that was the most important thing for her to hold on to. Except it made her sad. Because she was trying to embrace feeling more. Actually wanting more. Wanting everything. It was difficult to do that when he was reminding her at every turn just what reason she had to protect herself.

And she had already been hurt. That was a problem. She had been devastated by life. And it was so complicated with her father, because she didn't want to be whiny about that relationship, not when he meant well.

And he did.

He loved her, that was the thing. He wasn't a cold, unfeeling man. If he knew the ways in which he had made her insecure he would feel terrible about it. She knew that.

But she'd been hurt all the same.

And so she always tried to protect herself. To manage her expectations. To remind herself that everything would be fine today and could still go wrong tomorrow. What person who had experienced the more random side of life's cruelties at such a young age wouldn't do the same thing? But she really cared about him. And he made her feel things. Want things.

"I thought that I had love, but it didn't protect me. It didn't keep me safe. What was the purpose of it? It *lied* to me. My father lied to me. He failed me."

"But you won't fail our child," she said. "I know you won't. It isn't in you, Dario. It just isn't."

He shook his head. Once. Just once.

"I can't trust myself."

She wanted to deny it, instantly. "I have a very hard time believing that. You are a good man. And you're full of passion."

"I..."

And she realized that this was as far as he could go right now. And she needed to let it go. It wasn't like she could fall down to her knees and tell him that she loved him.

The idea made her feel disquieted. Because she was afraid that she was closer to that than she would like to be. "Your father bought this place for you, didn't he?"

"Yes," she said. Feeling very sharply aware that it was yet another thing that didn't really belong to her.

"Don't do that," he said. "Do not doubt yourself."

"I don't understand you," she said. "Because you made it very clear that nothing that you have done in the past couple of months was really all about me or for me. You tell me that you can't give me love. And then you don't want me to doubt myself."

"Because it's me," he said, deeply certain. "It isn't you. What you consider success to be. I trust nothing. I can't. Do you know..." He looked away from her, out the window. She was struck by his profile. He was such a beautiful man. Beautiful, troubled. Wounded.

"My father told me that we were going to meet some friends. But he lied. He did not know them. I think he did not know what they intended for me. I was to help. And nothing more. A servant. But I didn't know that at first. I believed my father. I trusted him. I never saw him again. He left me there. I should be grateful that all they made me do was scrub the floors. Do the farm chores. Because the alternative was selling my body. And they knew many people who did that. I saw so clearly that day what love means. Nothing. He said he loved me. As easily as if he was stepping out to have a cigarette. He never came back. He didn't know what they intended for me. And he left me. He didn't know. He didn't care. That would have been a profound betrayal. For any adult to grab a child by the hand in the street and subject them to such a thing would be a profound betrayal. But mine came at the hands of my own father. I will never understand."

She moved to him. Rested her head on his chest, then her hands. She could feel his heart thundering. Could feel the weight of all this inside him. She felt it in herself.

She wanted to fix it. She knew she couldn't. Not because in this she doubted herself or felt inadequate, but because she didn't know if there was a cure for the kind of horrendous pain he'd been put through by the person who was supposed to care for him.

"Neither will I," she whispered. "I promise you, I am going to love your child. And take care of him. I promise."

He wrapped his arms around her. And held her.

"I know. I will take care of you both. You have my word."

But not his love. She could understand it now. Just a little bit more. A little bit better. Why that word specifically felt loaded. Like a lie. One it didn't seem anyone said it to him since? She didn't have to ask that.

They hadn't.

She knew they hadn't. Her father barely said it to her, and often only did when she said it first, not because he didn't feel it, but because he wasn't an overly emotive man. He would never say it to Dario. He would say he was like a son to him, clap him on the shoulder. Hug him, as he had the other night. But he wouldn't freely say that he loved him. And so Dario had gone and challenged all this time, and he had to work through his own issues.

And he had come out the other side with them only partly worked through.

"I'm going to pack up my essentials," she said, moving away from him.

"I have staff to do that."

"We don't need staff, Dario. I'm happy to spend the day with you if you're happy to spend it with me."

And that was how she found herself packing with Dario looming around. Asking if she really needed to bring all these things.

It was amusing. A stark contrast to the heavy moment early. It was strange and wonderful they could share these things. The dark, the light and the in-between.

"When did you decide to leave that family?"

"I was there for four years," he said. "Mostly because I didn't know what else to do. I ran away. I lived on the streets for nearly a year after that. We were very near a large cruise ship harbor. And I started hanging around. I pretended I was older. Someone at the port helped me manufacture some papers."

Her mouth dropped open. "Is your name really Dario Rivelli?"

He smiled. "That is what the paperwork says."

"But is it your name?"

"It is now."

"You're kidding me. You live under an assumed identity?"

"More or less."

"I was called *boy* by the family that I lived with. I was called nothing by the people on the streets. And I was given a new identity at thirteen and I have clung to it ever since" He knew his own name. He just didn't want her to know it.

"So you sailed to America on a cruise ship."

"Yes. I did a few contracts. Three months doing passenger cruises. Mostly I did food service. I found I was quite good at it."

"I bet."

"I looked maybe seventeen. It was beneficial. Then the cruise company was moving the ship to sail from New York down to the Caribbean. I decided to sail over on the understanding that I would be continuing on. But instead I got off the ship. And I stayed in New York."

"Were you homeless in New York?"

"For a while. I moved between shelters, bus stations and the park. I managed to get myself a place in a very questionable part of the city. One room. No room for anything but a mattress. Shared bathroom down the hall. But it was mine. And you have no idea what that meant after everything."

"You're right," she said. "I don't. I can't. I've always had everything."

"But you're hurt by that comment," he said. "By pieces of your life anyway."

"I am."

"Amazing."

"Do you think I shouldn't be?"

He shook his head slowly. "No. That's not what I mean at all. Of course you can be hurt. I am only… I am turning over what that means for me."

"Did you think that you were healed?"

"I'm fine."

"Dario," she said. "You can't even speak your name to me. I don't think you're fine."

After that, they didn't speak much. They only packed up and made their way to his glorious Manhattan penthouse. It made her apartment look like a hovel. It was the entire top floor of the apartment building and overlooked the most brilliant views in New York. She imagined him coming here as a boy, and the way he must've looked up at these buildings. And the way he looked down now.

Looking at him, she knew that he had those exact thoughts. It wasn't an accident.

She had always seen Dario as difficult. And then as

someone inflexible who looked down on her. She had never seen him as wounded. Now she was forced to. He was still so very much that boy that had come here with nothing. And she wondered how many of the things he did were based on that. She had her own issues, that much was certain. But not like him. She'd always had safety. That was the biggest difference. They had both experienced loss. They both understood that pain. But he had experienced scarcity, fear, uncertainty. Abuse. She had never had to contend with any of that. And still she was affected. How much more so must he be?

It made her want to give to him. Because hadn't he given so much to her already?

He had seen something in her that she hadn't fully seen herself. Something she'd been hopeful about, but hadn't been certain of. He had told her without reservation that she was smart. That she was talented.

He hadn't denigrated her workspace. Hadn't called her disorganized. He seemed interested.

She wanted to figure out how to heal him. But she didn't know how.

Not really.

She came from a much easier background, and she couldn't sort through exactly how somebody like her could help somebody like him.

She wanted to, though. More than anything.

And if those feelings were maybe a little bit more, a little bit beyond what she wanted, what she wished, well, she was just going to have to deal with it. Because it was, absolutely, but it was.

Dario had been a fixture in her life for a long time. And now they were going to be married.

It was impossible to not have feelings.

She was going to ask him if she was going to have her own room.

But before she could get the words out, he leaned in and kissed her.

And then she found herself being carried off to his bedroom.

And the logistics just suddenly didn't matter anymore.

Because she was here with Dario.

And they were going to make a life together, whatever that looked like.

And she was going to find a way to give him whatever he needed.

CHAPTER THIRTEEN

HIS HOUSE HAD changed since Lyssia had moved in. He supposed that was somewhat inevitable. She wasn't a neat or contained person. She was an eclectic explosion of color. There were clothes on the floor of his house.

He had always kept things neat. He didn't like chaos. He experienced enough of it in his life. But Lyssia was a soft, pink sort of chaos, and he found that part of him could actually enjoy it. Relish it, even.

He found himself thinking often of their honeymoon. He had decided that after their wedding in Rome he would spirit her off to Tahiti. Take her to a private island and enjoy looking at her in various bathing suits. He would work on acquiring a collection of bikinis between now and then. Today they were having a bridal gown fitting, in his home.

And he had been ushered out of the room. As if it mattered. As if he shouldn't be allowed to see her. He had said something about the fact that tradition meant little when the bride was already pregnant. Lyssia had slapped him on the shoulder and shooed him away.

And so he was standing as an exile in his own

kitchen, drinking an espresso and wondering exactly how he had gotten here. He could recall that day when he had seen Lyssia in the chalet, and she had lost the entire contents of her suitcase.

He could recall, even then, the gnawing hunger he felt for her.

The way he was drawn to her.

And now she lived with him. Was marrying him.

She was on the verge of becoming… His family.

The word sat uncomfortably inside of him.

In some capacity, he had long thought of Nathan Anderson as a father figure. But there was a barrier. They were not family. Not really. Not truly. And now… Well. He and Lyssia would be family. Their child would be…

His heart felt like it had been grabbed and twisted.

He was having a child. A human that shared his DNA. Born of his blood.

He had lost his mother. His father had lost him.

He had not had a connection like that with another person in a long time.

Family.

Suddenly, and in so many ways. That traditional connection of marriage. That inevitable connection of blood.

And he knew that it was not simply blood that made a family. For if it did, the bond between him and his father could not have been broken, but it was. But still, it was a foundational connection, and one that forged a bond. It was up to him to not squander it. Up to him to do right by it.

He could figure out how to protect a child. But as

much as he loved his mother, there had been no way for him to protect her from cancer. She had gotten ill, and that wasn't his fault.

That was, perhaps, the deepest and most unresolved issue of his life. That his father had failed him so grandly, and he would love to put every failure on his father's shoulders. But he couldn't.

Because it had been something far beyond the control of men that had taken his mother away.

She had gotten treatment. In that sense, his father had done right by his wife.

He wanted to vow to protect his family, but how could he, when he knew that there were some things that were beyond control? How could he protect Lyssia when the world was full of accidents and illness?

She knew that as well.

The thought of all this made his chest ache, and perhaps what he resented most of all was how often this new turn of events in his life made him think of these things.

Lyssia had brought up the subject of his old name.

He didn't even think it. He would never say it out loud.

A moment later, he heard voices, and the door to Lyssia's bedroom opened. She and the dress designer exited.

"Are you pleased?" he asked.

"Yes," she said, her eyes shining bright. With the promise of what, he wondered. Was it a future with him that made her so happy? Or was it simply this momentary satisfaction of finding a bridal gown that she liked?

He found he wasn't sure, and in fact, wanted to know.

He wanted to be the source of that happiness.

And yet, at the same time, he couldn't bear the idea.

Because… Because of everything.

He thanked the designer, and so did Lyssia, and when the door had closed and the woman had left, Lyssia came into the kitchen and wrapped her arms around his neck, pressing her body to him and kissing him. He held her lightly. It was strange, these casual moments of affection. He was accustomed to the wild and untamed need between them. Sort of.

But this… The way she touched him. The way she would kiss him, just to kiss him.

It was all beyond him.

"I'm looking forward to the wedding," she said. "Everything is coming together."

"Have your invitations gone out?"

"Yes. My father has graciously chartered a plane to bring my friends over."

"Friends from university?"

"Yes. Obviously I'm bragging because I'm marrying a very sexy billionaire. Who can blame me?"

He did not have a plane full of friends to bring. He had business associates. People he had made connections with.

"Well, I'm very glad for you."

"Am I not your trophy wife, Dario? Much younger… Etcetera. Etcetera."

"You are not that much younger than me."

"Yes, I am," she said, grinning. "In fact, that's one reason he felt as if you had to rush to marry me. The scandal of it all. But surely on some level it must appeal to your male ego."

"My ego is just fine."

That much was true. He was not a man given to insecurity. That had been a luxury he could never quite afford.

She laughed and moved away from him. He wanted to have sex with her. Because she had kissed him like that. Because turning it into sex made it feel more manageable. Because turning it into sex made it feel like something more than just casual affection. And for some reason casual affection felt… Impossible.

But she was moving about like a whirlwind, collecting her things.

"I have to go down to one of my showrooms. There is an issue with some supply that we got, and I have to look into it. Thank God it's a limited collection and not something we're manufacturing for you or my father. I don't need new disasters on that large of a scale."

"You cannot stay?"

He heard the need in his own voice and he despised himself for it.

"No," she said. "I can't stay. I have work to do. I'm sure you do too."

He growled, and moved closer to her, taking her hand and pressing it to the front of his slacks. Her eyebrows lifted. "Oh, my. Well. I'm sure that will keep for me."

"I want you," he said.

"And I want you," she said. "Always. But I have a work emergency."

And for the first time in his life, Dario found himself abandoned, aroused, by a woman.

He was proud of her too. For her resolve. For the new strides she was making in her career, even while managing all of this.

But she'd left him with nothing more than the impression of her soft lips against his, and an aching need for more.

Along with the swirling, cavernous feeling of need that he was assaulted by.

A need to protect her when he knew the world would not always allow it. A need to have her so that he could exist in the space that was not consumed with his desire for her.

Dio, but it was unbearable.

And he had to sit with the unbearableness of it until she returned hours later. And then, only then did he have her. And have her he did. On the couch, in the shower. In his bed.

Until he erased the memory of affection and replaced it with lust. Until he blotted out those open-ended emotional concerns from earlier and spun them into sex. Because that at least he knew he was good at. That at least he knew he could give her. It was a connection that was real and strong.

And it was what he would lean on.

Because in that at least, he knew his power.

As for the vagaries of the rest of the world and fatherhood?

It was best not to ponder it too deeply.

CHAPTER FOURTEEN

ROME WAS SPECTACULAR. Lyssia couldn't recall the last time she had been there. She had been a child, she was pretty sure, and dragged on a business trip of her father's after her mother had died.

Most of her time in Italy had been spent in the northern part of the country, and while she had done a fair amount of traveling, there had never been much occasion to go to Rome.

She watched Dario's face as they descended on their private jet, and then even closer still as they drove through the city, so overcrowded and teeming with people.

"I can't believe you lived on the streets here," she said.

He flicked a glance at her. "I survived."

"Does this feel like home to you?"

"No. This was home to a boy long since dead."

And yet, she knew that wasn't true. He was Italian. This was part of who he was. He sought to deny it. Because it was painful. She knew what it was like, to wonder what could've been. She wondered if those thoughts consumed him now.

She didn't say anything, however.

Instead, she kept her peace until they arrived at the hotel they would be staying at. Gloriously appointed, and of course with the room on the top floor because Dario simply had to look down on the world.

He had been so trapped before. She really could understand.

Their connection had always been powerfully sexual. But he had been even more intense this past week. Every interaction between them ended with sex. She wasn't complaining, it was just that she could feel him trying to avoid something via their passion.

It made her feel terribly sad for him.

And for herself. Because she was still trying to figure out exactly what she could give him.

What he could get from her that he couldn't get from anywhere else.

Her father arrived in Rome later that day, and the three of them went and had dinner near the Colosseum. It was crowded and dizzying, but she enjoyed it. She liked even more listening to Dario speak Italian, translating easily for them, and becoming more relaxed as the evening wore on.

He was relaxed, and she hadn't thought he would be. Whenever tension crept up in him, when they crossed a certain street, or the wind changed, she touched his hand. He would relax again. And she liked the feeling he was able to be happy here partly because of her.

I will have wealth, my wife and my child.

He'd said that about Rome. Perhaps this was what he'd needed to face it again. To feel different enough.

He was a fascinating man.

Brilliant. Exceptional.

Handsome.

It grieved her that his father had betrayed him. That he had thrown him away like so much garbage when…

Imagining him as a small boy, confused and left behind, filled her with aching sorrow. If they had a little boy, and he had dark eyes just like his father, she would hurt every time she looked at him for that small boy Dario had been. Left behind and left without love.

And she would give their son love doubly in response.

She couldn't explain it. But she knew it was going to be a boy. She just knew she was carrying Dario's son.

She blinked back impending tears that threatened to fall.

She kept on smiling. Because the moment was happy. Even if it was weighted with other things.

The night before the wedding she took up residence in a different hotel room, much to Dario's chagrin.

In the next morning, she felt completely undone, her heart fluttering continually, her hand shaking as her team of stylists got her ready.

She had chosen the dress because it reminded her of her mother. Her mother had always told her stories about the Fae Folk. And the soft gown with its plunging neckline and sleeves that trailed down along with the train reminded her of fairies. Elves. Something otherworldly.

She left her hair loose, with long ringlets. And she hoped that he would think she was beautiful. Her makeup was done expertly. Soft and natural to make her glow, but little more.

Her bouquet was made of cascading lilies, and she knew that the old church they were marrying in would be filled with candelabras and draped in flowers.

She had deliberately kept all of this from Dario, because she felt it fitting for the groom to be surprised.

Also, she hadn't wanted his opinion. He wasn't the one with design aesthetic. She was.

She got into the car that was waiting to take her to the church, and pressed her bouquet to her breast.

She was trying to calm the beating of her heart, or perhaps she just wanted to feel it.

She looked out at the city, and slowly, with each turn of the tires on the road, she realized something.

She wasn't marrying Dario for the sake of their child. In truth, she never had been.

She could've fought him on this. It would've been easy.

She had power, and her relationship with her father mattered to Dario, because his relationship with her father mattered.

She was not marrying him because he had forced her into it. Because he had coerced or blackmailed her in any way. She was marrying him because she wanted to.

The car pulled up to the church and her father was standing outside waiting for her, wearing a suit. The door opened and he reached his hand out, lifting her from the back of the car. His eyes were shining. "Lyssia," he said softly. "You are a beautiful bride."

That tenuous grasp on her emotional stability eroded, and she found herself crying and being thankful for waterproof makeup.

"Dad," she said. "I..."

She expected him to say something about how proud he was, because she was marrying Dario. Instead, he looked down at her, blue eyes sparkling. "I am amazed at the woman you've become. You're not a child anymore, and I know that. You haven't been one for quite some time. But I have always been reluctant to let go of you as my little girl. You're the only child that I have. I think sometimes I have not given you all the credit you deserve simply because I couldn't bear the idea that you were grown. I wanted you to need me. To need my advice. Perhaps even to need to work for my company because I wanted to keep you close. But you don't need that. You are an incredible person. Smart and ambitious. But far warmer than I've ever been. You are more like your mother that way. Your softness. Your creativity. She would be overjoyed today."

"It's been hard, Dad," she whispered. "There have been a lot of times I haven't felt like...like I mattered."

He closed his eyes. He looked pained. For the first time she realized he knew. And much the same way she'd been afraid to ask him for what she wanted, he'd been afraid to examine his failures. To hear them spoken out loud. Because they would no longer be doubts, they'd be confirmed.

"I am sorry," he said. "For all the things I didn't

do when you were young. For all the things I couldn't give you, even when you deserved them. I am sorry."

"You don't have to be sorry," she said. "You're a good father."

"But you have not always felt loved, I don't think."

Bittersweetness lanced her chest. "No," she said. "I have always felt loved. Sometimes I didn't feel like you were proud of me. Sometimes I didn't feel like you understood me. But I always knew that you loved me, Dad. I never doubted that. I did think maybe you loved Dario a little bit more."

"I do love Dario," he said. "He is the son I never had. The son I never could've had. I never wanted anyone other than your mother. Not to live with. Not to have children with. He felt like a blessing because without him, there never would've been another child. You see? And now you're giving me a grandchild, with him. It is a gift. But it's not what I needed to be proud of you. And I don't need you to be like him."

"Thank you," she said.

"It was never that I didn't love you as much," he said. "I loved you so much it felt like breaking apart, and the only thing that ever felt like that was loving and losing your mother. I…never avoided you because you weren't enough."

"Oh, Dad." She wrapped her arms around him. It didn't erase his mistakes. But she loved him. He loved her. It was enough.

Part of her felt healed in that moment. She was enough. She always had been.

It was just that sometimes her father didn't show

his feelings. And she didn't show hers. It was all part of being afraid of the ways the world would hurt you, she supposed.

Her father led her into the church, and toward the sanctuary.

They waited. Waited for their cue. And then the wedding coordinator signaled them, and the doors opened. And when she saw Dario standing there at the head of the aisle, suddenly she knew. She knew exactly what she needed to give him.

Love.

And right then she had the confidence in that. And the fact that her love mattered. And that it would mean something.

And it was also the moment when she knew, deep in her soul, that today she was marrying Dario because she loved him.

And that was the only reason.

Love.

When he saw Lyssia, the breath exited his body.

She was ethereal. An angel, on the arm of her father. Her dress was made of floating, diaphanous white fabric that rode around her like a cloud with each step she took. Her breasts were round and lush, highlighted by the low neckline.

Her face glowed, the joy there a sight so beautiful he nearly had to look away. Because he hardly deserved it.

Hardly deserved that bright, beautiful brilliance that she shone his way.

And when her father released his hold on her and

passed her to Dario, he felt a brilliant weight of responsibility come down upon his shoulders.

She looked up at him with absolute trust in her eyes, took his hands, and they began their exchange of vows.

He spoke each one with heavy truth. Because whatever he had said in the beginning, he now intended to honor these vows. Forever. Forsaking all others, for as long as they lived.

He could not explain the intensity of this, he only knew it consumed him. Changed him. Became the essence of who he was.

In that moment, he became Lyssia's husband, as she became Dario's wife.

It seemed absurd that only a few months ago, it had taken a blizzard, and the lack of some boy in his twenties for the two of them to become what they were.

For they seemed to stretch beyond the fabric of time. Had there ever been a moment when Lyssia was not his? He could not recall it. Not truly.

The faces of the people in the crowd blurred before him. And he could see nothing but her.

They were married. He had spoken vows. There was, he came to realize, a reception planned for after the wedding, but the entire thing tried his patience. He didn't want a party. He wanted to be alone with her.

She danced with her friends, and with her father. He danced with her, but everything in him was demanding that he make her his in the most elemental way.

At first there was a cake. And he was thankful for the years he had spent learning charm, because he had to call upon all of those years now so that he could get through it with his humor intact.

She tossed her beautiful bouquet, and right after that he swept her away to the airport. To his private jet. They should've stayed an extra night in Rome, but he had been desirous to get her away from everyone and everything. To have her all to himself. So now they had a long flight overnight to the private island.

She was exhausted. And so he helped her out of her gown and did not ravish her as he wanted, but left her sleeping in the bedroom alone while he drank to try and drown the intensity of everything.

Sex helped him make sense of the intensity. When he was inside of her, when he was chasing the peak of need, then they could make all of that about sex.

But now, the ache in his chest felt like it was something else, and he did not care for it at all.

After this, they would return home. A home that they shared. They would have a baby.

A child together.

Their lives were being knit together as yarn becoming something new.

And he had never imagined that would be so.

Not for him.

It was like having a version of his past resurrected. A set of new choices given to him.

And this wild need that he felt for Lyssia terrified him, because it compromised everything that he had ever told himself about connection.

About the decision he had made to marry her. And why it had been important. It had been about his child.

Of course it had been. About the need to make sure they were both protected, but it didn't feel like it now.

It didn't feel like a decision made coolly with his mind and nothing more.

His feelings for Lyssia felt nothing like logic.

Nothing like himself.

He brooded on that all night, and when they touched down on the island, Lyssia emerged looking fresh, while he felt as if he had run a gauntlet.

"This is beautiful," she said as they walked up the trail that led to the home they would be staying in. Gorgeous and open to the jungle around them, because there were no other people to disturb them. The house was fully stocked, overlooking the water. There was a private dock with a small boat that they could take out at their leisure.

But he wanted none of that. Not now. He wanted nothing other than to have her. Nothing other than to make her his.

And when they arrived at the house, he did not wait to get inside. He grabbed hold of her on the sundeck and kissed her, deep and hard. Then he laid her down across one of the luxurious outdoor beds and began to strip her of all her clothes.

She was beautiful. Beyond.

Everything he had ever desired.

He had known. From that first moment in his office, he had known.

That whatever she had been to him before, she had become the woman of his dreams.

Dreams he hadn't even known he possessed.

He stripped her body and as he did, stripped layers of himself away. Of his protections. And he found he did not have the desire to resist. Either her or the need between them.

He sipped desire from between her legs and kissed his way back up her body. Sucking one nipple into his mouth and reveling in the intensity of what bloomed between them.

He had been alone. For so many years, he had been alone. And now he was with her. In a way he had never been. Never been with anyone.

She had gotten underneath his skin. She had gotten down to the very heart of who he was.

Something he wasn't entirely sure he had known before.

But she made him want to be better.

She made him want everything. And when he slid into her tight body, he felt himself coming home.

It was not wrong. It never could be. It was not an apartment at the top of the world.

Home, very quickly, had become this year, and that felt like a very dangerous thing.

But he couldn't turn away from it, not now. He was a slave to it. To her. He could do nothing but ride them both to the end. To completion.

But carry them both away on a cloud of desire. Because this was where it made sense. And this was where he could show her. It was where he would be able to manage this, because outside of this moment, outside of her body, it felt like a terrible thing. Great and awful, and like four walls and a home in Rome that he never wanted to revisit. Like a name he couldn't say, like a heart he could never allow to beat again. No. It had to be this. It could only ever be this. Always and forever.

"Dario," she said, shuddering out her pleasure as he found his own. As he shouted out his completion.

They clung to each other. And in the aftermath, he could hear only the sound of their hearts, and the waves.

"Dario," she said softly, looking up at him, those familiar blue eyes an integral part of the story of his life. "I love you."

And the world shattered.

CHAPTER FIFTEEN

LYSSIA KNEW THAT it would be the harder road. She did. But she hadn't been able to hold back. Not anymore. Because the truth was, she loved him. And the truth was, she was certain that the only way forward was to allow herself to love him. Fully and openly. Because the only way she was ever going to reach him. The only way she was ever going to change him, was through that love.

She knew it as much as she knew that the ocean was out there, fathomless and blue. She knew it as much as she knew anything.

She had needed it to be said. Because she needed to let herself feel it. Without reservation. There was fear. But she had spent all of her life holding herself back. Out of fear. Out of the fear that she would find herself alone again, unloved.

She wasn't going to hold back, not anymore.

Never again.

There was no scope for fear.

Not when she loved him like she did. Not when she

felt a burning desire to not simply be changed by him, but to change him in return.

He was, and had been, the most incredible influence on her life these past months. And even before that. He had made her feel a spirit of competition, and while she had resented that at times, she couldn't deny that it had driven her.

He had, without even meaning to, created a better version of Lyssia.

She wanted to make a better version of Dario.

What he had lost in his life, it was love. That was the thing that had felt tenuous to him. It was the thing that had felt conditional. The thing that had felt like a betrayal, and she had to make it steady. She had to make it real. She had to take the love and make it enduring. And it was terrifying, of course it was. Because she understood how random the world could be, she understood loss. She knew what it was like to feel like everything was fine one moment then have it be wrenched away the next, but she couldn't live in that space. Because they were going to have a child. And she had to love that child completely and wholly. With all of herself.

She had to find it within her to give that child love unreservedly, and it began here. Her father had loved her mother, so much. And even though he had been grief stricken in the years since he had lost her, she also knew that he wouldn't change a thing. She didn't even have to ask that. He was, now and ever, abundantly clear on what that love had meant to him. On how impacting it had been.

Love was not the enemy. It was fear.

Plain and simple. It was what had destroyed Dario's childhood. And it was what would continue to destroy him if she wasn't the brave one.

And she would be. At the expense of everything.

He said nothing. Because of course that was quintessentially Dario. To just ignore her, to pretend it hadn't happened. Rather than rounding on her or being cruel.

"I said that I love you," she said, drawing her knees up to her chest.

"I heard you," he said, his voice hard.

"Yes, well, you didn't acknowledge it, and many people might find that grounds for assuming they had been unheard." It was warm outside. As hot now as it had been cold at the chalet. When they had sat by the fireplace and shared sausages. When things had felt simpler.

Except… They felt more real now. More consequential.

They felt terrifying.

The stakes had never been higher. And none of the wedding guests even knew about the pregnancy.

"I don't know what response you're looking for," he said.

"There is the usual response to that question, Dario."

"I told you what love was to me. Or rather, what it wasn't. I am not the person that you're looking for. Not in this."

"What if I told you I'm not actually looking for anything? What if I told you I was offering you love? And that is not an action item. You can take it, or you can simply let it sit there, but it doesn't change the fact that I love you."

He looked… Lost then. Sad and desperate. "Why? Why do you love me?"

It killed her. Because he didn't know. She could see that. She could feel it, that emptiness in him echoing in her.

She put her hand on his chest.

"Because you have made me see parts of myself that I didn't before. Because you are a good man, and I've seen it."

She thought of all that good while she said it. The way he encouraged her. The way he believed in her.

"Because you are strong in the face of great adversity, and because you know when to be soft, too. You have been with me. Whether you realize it or not. Because no matter how hard I try, I seem to not be able to stay away from you. Because you have introduced me to new aspects of my body, but of my soul too. You have made me a deeper person."

She didn't even recognize the girl who had come to the chalet that had thought she had it all figured out. "You have made me a better person. I'm going to be a mother because of you. Because of us. It is really not overstating it to say that you're the single most important person in my life. That you have been for a very long time. I was running from you. That day that I showed up to the chalet with a suitcase full of lingerie, waiting for another man. I was running from you. I knew that you were the one that I needed. But I also knew that you were never going to be easy. Because a man who fought as hard as you did to get above all of that was never going to be easy. So I'm not asking you for anything. I'm just giving."

"I don't understand," he said, his voice rough. "Who loves someone without getting love in return?"

"That's what love is. It's not a transaction. It's not conditional. It's not yours to give when it's easy. It's not about convenience. And I know that you weren't taught that. Not in your life. I know that your father betrayed you. That he betrayed your trust. And I am so, so very sorry. But I will not love you that way. I will not love you when it's easy and convenient, and when I am getting enough out of it to call it sufficient. I love you because of everything that you are. You have already given enough to me. You are already enough."

"How can that be?" he asked.

"You said it yourself," she said, her heart breaking, just a bit. "I told you I wanted a summer rain kiss. You told me I needed a hurricane. This is the whole hurricane, Dario. I'm already in it. And I don't want anything else."

"I also told you, you wanted the villain. I'm the villain of the story, *cara*, not your hero."

"No," she said. "That was where you got it wrong. I never wanted the villain. But I wanted real. I wanted complicated. I didn't want a man who existed to make me feel better about myself. I wanted a man who made me better. And that's you."

"You are very young," he said.

It was so dismissive, and she knew he was doing

it on purpose. Pushing her away. She wasn't going to let him.

"So what? Maybe that's what you need. Somebody young enough that they haven't done this before and they aren't afraid." She put her hands on his face and stared at him. "Because I know that it's going to take a lot of energy, but I have it. More than that, I need it. I can't keep part of myself back from you while giving everything to our child. I know that I can't. I have to open it all up. Slice into the vein and let it all just bleed out."

"You don't know what you're asking for…"

"Maybe I do. So here we are. This is what I have to give, and I know that it's good enough. And the reason I know it is good enough is because you have made me feel like I'm enough. So if you want to blame someone for this, blame yourself. A few months ago I would never have thought that this was a gift. My love. I would've laughed about that. Because what about my love could possibly be a gift? I just saw myself as a silly little rich girl. I know I see myself as a lot more. Because of you. I know that I deserve more. I know that we deserve more. We deserve everything. We don't deserve to be defined by our hardships. By the things that we've lost. We simply don't. We deserve everything. We deserve love."

He was reeling, and she could see that.

"We are on our honeymoon. I promise you this isn't conditional. I want to be on our honeymoon. I don't want to push you away. All I've ever wanted is to bring you closer."

"I don't need love," he said.

"You're wrong. It's the one thing that you need, more than anything. You have billions, and you're still broken. You have billions and you still can't face the boy that you were. It's the one piece of yourself you haven't yet repaired. Your heart, Dario. Let me."

"Thank you, Lyssia," he said. "You are offering something I simply don't require. It isn't you. It isn't that you were wrong or insufficient. It is me. I simply don't need it. And I won't ask to hear it again. I can't."

And with that, he walked away from her, naked, each beautiful line of his body a rejection of what she had offered.

She sat there, the warm breeze blowing through her hair.

They were married. She knew him. He wasn't going to leave her. But he was going to wall himself off. Make himself a stranger. Pull away.

She thought perhaps she wouldn't see him for the whole rest of the honeymoon. Instead, he became voracious.

He made love to her multiple times a day, but he didn't speak to her after. And she allowed it. She let him soothe himself with her body, and each and every time she gave everything.

This was a real test of her strength. Of her endurance.

Because this was love rejected.

And if he had left her, then perhaps she could begin the cycle of healing. But they would never have separation. She would love him, alone. Isolated. And that was what she had offered. She had done it feeling like eventually he would come around. But he didn't. He was somehow distant and more near at the same time. And when they finished their two weeks on the island, they traded in all that sundrenched beauty for the gloom of Manhattan, for a shared space but not a shared life in a house in Midtown.

They didn't talk. Not often.

She felt like she had lost an integral part of him. Because what she had lost was their connection. The one that they had before sex. The one that they'd always had. He had always been there.

She didn't invite him to her doctor appointments, because why?

The months melted together. Everything melted together.

And finally it was time for her to go and get her ultrasound where they could find out the gender of the baby. She knew that she wasn't going to actually speak to Dario until she texted him, to tell him that he could come to the appointment if he wanted to.

She didn't expect a response. But when she arrived at the doctor's office, he appeared. Looking every inch the thunder.

"Oh," she said. "I didn't expect you to actually show up."

"You invited me," hc said.

They were ushered into the room right away, which was plush and glorious, and a perk, she knew, of her marriage.

They weren't kept waiting for long before an ultrasound technician came into the room.

"If you can undress and lie down I'll be back in a moment," the woman said.

Lyssia obeyed, and lay back on the table. She said nothing to Dario.

"I'm surprised you asked me," he said.

"Why? I'm not the one who made it weird. I just said that I loved you. You're the one that got distant. You're the one that quit talking to me."

"And you're the one that got upset when I refused to give you what I had said that I couldn't, and then you said it was offered freely. But you're angry. Why did you invite me if you find me so confounding?"

"Because I wanted you here."

The woman came back a moment later, and they stopped their discussion. She put gel on Lyssia's stomach, and that familiar watery sound filled the room. She'd had more than one scan and several Doppler appointments, so she had become somewhat familiarized with the state of her womb.

Still, she held her breath a little bit each time. Waiting for the heartbeat. Waiting for the definitive proof that her baby was still there. Still with her. She could feel it move now, a little bit. And she was the one who had chosen not to share that with Dario. So in that sense, he was right. She had offered to continue to love him, as if it was all the same, and she had become wounded about the whole thing.

But then, the heartbeat echoed in the room, and she

could see their baby's profile. "Oh," she said. "There he is."

Dario looked confused. "He?"

"I just have a feeling. But we don't know yet."

"We will soon," said the ultrasound tech. "Provided the baby is not shy."

"He won't be," said Dario.

They were both so certain that when the ultrasound tech found the anatomy she was looking for and said, "It's a boy," Lyssia only smiled. "I knew it. I knew it was your son."

But Dario stood up, and suddenly looked pale. Ashen. And then he walked out of the room, leaving Lyssia sitting there staring at the ultrasound tech.

"Is he okay?" the woman asked.

"No. I think he has a load of childhood trauma that he isn't quite sure how to work through. But I'm going to need him to start doing it."

Dario was out on the streets. The high-rise looming over him, and people wandering all around him. It was like when he'd come here for the first time. It was like when he'd been a boy. Lost in the shuffle, lost in the madness. It was everything he was afraid of. Everything he had escaped.

A son.

He had known that there was a possibility of that, and had even felt certain along with Lyssia when she had said that. A son.

A little dark-eyed boy who would be like him.

It wrenched him. Tore him open.

He was going to have to relive this. Have to revisit it, and there was no getting away from it. He had made a decision to care for his son. But right then, he knew it wasn't enough. He knew he wasn't enough.

Lyssia had stood there, with truth shining out from her eyes when she had said that she now understood she was enough. Always, and forever. That her love was sufficient. How did he get there? How?

He knew the answer. But he hated the answer. He had to demolish the walls inside of himself, he didn't have another choice. He had to tear it all down. He had to find a way.

But the only way to do it was to make himself vulnerable, and the thought of that made him…

They lived in a home together. Happy home. And God, he had one of those before, and it had been wrenched away from him. It was hideous. To love someone as he had, and to lose her. And worse still, to love his father as he had and lose him.

To have him choose to walk away. Could he love Lyssia? Could he love his son?

Would it be enough?

How can you not?

Of course he had to. Of course he did. He couldn't breathe. He couldn't think.

Why was he wandering the streets like a homeless child? Why did he feel like a homeless child?

He was the same boy he'd always been.

Raphael.

He pushed that away. That name. That part of himself.

Raphael.

He was him again.

He had not escaped.

He was out there, alone. Abandoned.

And then he turned, and he saw her. Walking down the sidewalk, and it was as the crowd parted. Lyssia. Still coming for him. Even when he didn't deserve it.

"Dario," she said. "What… What's wrong?"

"A son," he said. "I will have a wife and a son, and I will fail him. I will fail you. I don't know… My father loved my mother too much, and then he couldn't bear it when she died. How can I be a good father, and a good husband?"

"Because you can withstand it. Because you can withstand it all. Because that is who you are. But I don't believe life will ask that from us."

"What if it does?"

"You will be the man you've become. In the face of everything. And so will I. It was not love that was weak when your father let you go. And deep down I think you know that."

"He did not love me. Not really."

"Or perhaps he didn't love himself. Perhaps he didn't see a way out. But it was his fear that won. Not his love. And it was not his love for your mother that caused him to do that, because if he truly loved her, if in that moment he could truly feel what he had felt for her when she was alive, he never would have left her son. I would kill you. I would come back and haunt your ass so hard, Dario. If you abandoned our child? No. Your tribute, your love for me would inspire you to be the best father you could be. My father did that.

Even if imperfectly. And I am well, in spite of his imperfections. Love does not have to be perfect. It simply must endure."

"I do love you," he said, everything within him trembling now. "I do. But I am… I am afraid. Because I feel closer to the boy that I was now than I ever have been. I feel perilously close to losing everything."

"You've always been that boy. That boy is the one that got you here. Don't hate him. He was strong enough to bring you where you needed to go. He was strong enough to help turn you into the man that I love."

"I love you," he said.

"It means more here, doesn't it? Down in the street."

He nodded. "It reminds me of then. I… I." He took a breath and looked at her. "I spent three hundred and sixty-seven days on the street. Every night when I went to sleep I was afraid."

"Oh, Dario…"

"I dreamed of having a bed, but there wasn't one. I dreamed of rescue, but I couldn't find it. I was cold, scared, alone. And I was eaten up with hatred for my father. I knew he would not rescue me so I found the strength to rescue myself."

"Dario, our son will never need rescuing. We'll already be there."

They would be. Always. He knew it, with all of his heart. This was love. And it had been, from the moment she'd spilled coffee in his office and he'd seen the woman she'd become, and it had changed him. It had been, slowly, in all the years since.

Every fight, every battle, had begun to tear at the layers of defense he'd put up. She was the only one he'd never tried to charm. She was the only one who knew him.

And he knew it was time.

"I was born Raphael Vicente. I made vows to you as Dario. And now I make them as Raphael. I will stay with you, honor you, and love you. With all of me."

A sob racked her frame and she threw herself into his arms. "Raphael," she whispered. "I feel like I always knew you. Like I knew him."

He held her tightly, emotion cascading over him in a wave. "Because you were the only one who looked at me and saw the truth. Saw it all."

She smiled through her tears. "It's mutual. You saw me when I didn't."

"You are kisses in a summer rain, Lyssia. And a whole hurricane besides. You are everything. You are mine, and I am yours. With you, I lose control and feel more grounded all at once. With you, I'm not afraid anymore. Not of love, not of the future, not of those three hundred and sixty-seven nights. With you, there is only love. Always."

She nodded gravely, and then she took his hands, as if they were making vows then and there. Again. "And I will stay with you. I will. Always. I promise." She leaned in, pressing her mouth to his. "You told me once you were what the world needed, spontaneously created to fill a void. But I don't think so. You weren't for the world. You were for me. You were never the villain, Dario. You were always my hero. From the very beginning."

Dario Rivelli had very expensive custom-made shoes, and for the first time in his life he did not have a plan. Instead, he was filled entirely with nothing beyond love. For the woman in front of him. And he knew that he needed to know nothing. Except for them. Except for this. And so he would. Always.

EPILOGUE

When their son was born, the joy that Lyssia felt was so far beyond any pain she had ever suffered it was like a beacon of light that changed everything around her. The entire world.

But then, that seemed to happen, daily, since falling in love with Dario.

They were in a private hospital suite, looking down at their baby. Her father had been brought to tears by the enormity of seeing his grandson.

A little boy with black hair and dark eyes, just like his father.

"Have you thought of the name yet?" She looked up at her husband, who hadn't taken his eyes off his son from the moment he had entered the world.

"I want… I want to name him Raphael," he said.

Tears stung her eyes. "You do? That will not be too painful for you?"

"All of this is pain in the most beautiful way. Because it is real. Because this is all that was meant to be. Because this is love. At its deepest and most powerful. Because it is everything. And I aim to change the story. The story of Raphael. He will be a boy that is loved. Always. From beginning to end. From here to all of eternity. He will be smart and ingenious like his mother. And like his father. But he will not have to strive. And when there is hardship, we will be there for him. We will make mistakes, because love is never perfect. But there will be love."

"Yes," she whispered. "There will be. Always."

And that much she knew was true. Because if there was one thing she had seen in her own life, through loss, and through mistakes and imperfections, it was that love, when given without fear, did in fact endure. It was in the memories of her mother, and the joy of her father. It was in the glow that existed between herself and Dario. It was in the deepest part of her soul.

And it shone so much brighter than fear ever could.

"Raphael Rivelli. I like it. And for his middle name?"

"Nathan," Dario said.

She smiled. "Raphael Nathan Rivelli. A tribute. To the life you should have had, and the man who loves us both."

"I am grateful for your father. I wonder if I could've found my way to this without him. Without his example."

"I think you could have. Although I'm grateful that you had him."

"Why is that?"

"Because true love always wins. And that's what we have. True love."

* * * * *

If you just couldn't put down
The Italian's Pregnant Enemy
be sure to check out these other fabulous
Maisey Yates stories!

A Bride for the Lost King
Crowned for His Christmas Baby
The Secret That Shocked Cinderella
Forbidden to the Desert Prince
A Virgin for the Desert King

Available now!

COMING NEXT MONTH FROM

HARLEQUIN

PRESENTS

#4177 CINDERELLA'S ONE-NIGHT BABY

by Michelle Smart

A glamorous evening at the palace with Spanish tycoon Andrés? Irresistible! Even if Gabrielle knows this one encounter is all the guarded Spaniard will allow himself. Yet, when the chemistry simmering between them erupts into mind-blowing passion, the nine-month consequence will tie her and Andrés together forever...

#4178 HIDDEN HEIR WITH HIS HOUSEKEEPER

A Diamond in the Rough

by Heidi Rice

Self-made billionaire Mason Foxx would never forget the sizzling encounter he had with society princess Bea Medford. But his empire comes first, always. Until months later, he gets the ultimate shock: Bea isn't just the housekeeper at the hotel he's staying at—she's also carrying his child!

#4179 THE SICILIAN'S DEAL FOR "I DO"

Brooding Billionaire Brothers

by Clare Connelly

Marriage offered Mia Marini distance from her oppressive family, so Luca Cavallaro's desertion of their convenient wedding devastated her, especially after their mind-blowing kiss! Then Luca returns with a scandalous proposition: risk it all for a no-strings week together...and claim the wedding night they never had!

#4180 PREGNANCY CLAUSE IN THEIR PAPER MARRIAGE

by Kate Hewitt

Honoring the strict rules of his on-paper marriage, Christos Diakis has fought hard to ignore the electricity simmering between him and his wife, Lana. Her request that they have a baby rocks the very foundations of their union. And Christos has neither the power—nor wish—to decline...

HPCNMRA0124

#4181 THE FORBIDDEN BRIDE HE STOLE

by Millie Adams

Hannah will do *anything* to avoid the magnetic pull of her guardian, Apollo, including marry another. Then Apollo shockingly steals her from the altar, and a dangerous flame is ignited. Hannah must decide—is their passion a firestorm she can survive unscathed, or will it burn everything down?

#4182 AWAKENED IN HER ENEMY'S PALAZZO

by Kim Lawrence

Grace Stewart never expected to inherit a palazzo from her beloved late employer. Or that his ruthless tech mogul son, Theo Ranieri, would move in until she agrees to sell! Sleeping under the same roof fuels their agonizing attraction. There's just one place their standoff can end—in Theo's bed!

#4183 THE KING SHE SHOULDN'T CRAVE

by Lela May Wight

Promoted from spare to heir after tragedy struck, Angelo can't be distracted from his duty. Being married to the woman he has always craved—his brother's intended queen—has him on the precipice of self-destruction. The last thing he needs is for Natalia to recognize their dangerous attraction. If she does, there's nothing to stop it from becoming all-consuming...

#4184 UNTOUCHED UNTIL THE GREEK'S RETURN

by Susan Stephens

Innocent Rosy Bloom came to Greece looking for peace. But there's nothing peaceful about the storm of desire tycoon Xander Tsakis unleashes in her upon his return to his island home! Anything they share would be temporary, but Xander's dangerously thrilling proximity has cautious Rosy abandoning all reason!